"Hello?"

"Hello."

"This is Joel. Mari's friend."

"Oh." Decision time. Should she date him, or stall, or refuse, or what, and whatever she did, would Mari care? Face it, all she knew about the man was what Dean had said: he was superrich and had sampled and dropped every one of Mari's top models.

He was speaking. "The Aegean, Greek place, Eighth Avenue and First. Eight o'clock. Work for you? OK?"

She hesitated.

Click!

Shit! What if it wasn't OK? Just like that and click? Name, time and place and not another word? Who did he think he was, the prick? Leaving her looking at her cell phone and feeling helpless and stupid.

Betsy put her cell phone back in her purse. That's exactly what he was, a prick. Probably thought of himself as a big prick, which was not exactly what Betsy needed, no, not after being dumped by the love of her life. But Dean and Mari were pretty much her only New York friends, and Mari was trying to cheer her up, and Mari wouldn't have fixed her up with this, this, whatever he was, unless she thought there might be something for Betsy in it.

It was raining all day long with the temperature in the fifties and Betsy alternated between angry and nervous, and then angry because she was nervous, and angry because she hadn't phoned Mari and crapped out, or at least threatened to do it and let Mari know she was thinking of it. Oh, face it, girl, what the hell, she was nervous because she was on her own in a new and very, very big and cold place but dammit she should be able to handle that, and him, whoever and whatever he was. And anyhow Mari and Dean would stand by her for sure unless she threw a drink in his face or something wild like that and why should she even be thinking thoughts like that? What was the matter with her?

The matter was she had nothing to wear. Her one expensive black would be out of place in a Greek dump in a red light nowhere. Red. She reached for her red dress. Nobody ever wore red at night and Mari would be furious. Fuck her. At least she had a new Burberry, Betsy did, and with the Goddam rain, she would need it. Shouldn't he have sent a car for her? A cab if not a limo? He was rich, and Mari must have told him something about Betsy's circumstances. Maybe that was de rigeur New York, in a foursome each makes his own way. She would call a cab herself, dammit. With the rain, she would have to call early.

She did, and the cabbie phoned on time, even if he didn't speak English, and at least he was waiting out there on the street. Betsy handed him the address on a piece of paper.

"You don' wanna go there," he said.

"It's a restaurant. You can drop me right out front."

He shrugged.

There was no Aegean restaurant at Eighth and Third, and no Greek restaurant with any name, either there or in the block, or in the next block in either direction. Five minutes, ten, went by. She tried phoning information and was put on hold. The cabbie went up Eighth to First street, down First past Poly Prep to Prospect Park, down Prospect Park past the toy place, the pre-school and the book store, back up Fourth because Third was one way, across Eighth Avenue past Sotto Voce, it was not there, turning right on Seventh, this was ridiculous, should she phone Mari or what, across Third Street,--and there it was! The Aegean Restaurant.

And of course it really started to pour while she was still paying the cabbie, and the tip, what do you tip in New York, ten percent, fifteen percent? She tipped fifteen and a little more, opened the door, opened her umbrella and made a run for it, clutching the umbrella close so it wouldn't blow out, and it didn't and she made it!

Dean was standing, and so was whatshisname, Joel, that was it, good looking man, smiling, and she liked the way he was looking at her while Dean kissed her on the cheek and performed the introductions. He was reaching for her, Joel, not trying to shake hands, oh, her coat and her umbrella. She slipped them off and stooped to kiss Mari as he, whatshisname, Joel said, "Stunning," and took her things to the check room.

What was stunning? Betsy, or her dress? The dress, obviously. Still, that was quick and unexpected. "Stunning" wasn't something she would have expected from him.

Betsy and Dean sat.

"He likes you," said Mari and Dean grinned.

"Shut up," Mari snapped at him.

Dean laughed and Joel returned to the table clutching the check from the coatroom. "Would you like me to hold it?"

No, and Betsy took it from his hand. Good looking man. Nice smile. Betsy realized she was smiling.

"Please accept my apologies for my really dumb directions," Joel said.

"I was afraid you'd drown in the rain," Dean said. "Mari kept phoning and phoning to tell you it was not Eighth but Seventh."

"Your cell phone was busy," Mari said.

"I was dialing information," Betsy said, and instantly felt stupid as Dean grinned.

Joel said, "But you're here and it's a promising beginning." His smile broadened. "Drink?" he said.

"Martini," Betsy said.

"Gin?" said Joel, waving for the waiter as he asked.

"Tanqueray," Betsy said.

"Mine," said Joel.

Dean said, "Betsy or the gin?"

"Oh, for Chrissake," Mari said to him.

But Betsy and Joel were smiling as he ordered the drinks, hers first, his second. Dean and Mari ordered Manhattans, with one cherry, black Jack.

"I can take care of myself," Betsy said to Dean.

"Hmm." Joel was murmuring.

"What?" said Betsy.

"I know you can," said Joel, immediately, "but I was just thinking."

"What?" she said again.

"Nothing," he said.

The drinks arrived. They were perfect. Nothing quite like the first

Martini sip and Betsy was instantly happy.

The dinner was good, they ordered wine, red and white, and the conversation was riveting, like one of those good movie oldies, the new books, the market, the new proposals by the mayor, and everyone's favorite cities. Betsy went quiet as the others spoke of London, Istanbul, Saigon, Hong Kong before and Hong Kong after.

"Did I ever tell you about meeting Truman Capote in Harry's Bar in Venice?" said Dean.

"And you slugged him when he hit on you. Yes, we've all heard it," Mari shot him down.

"I've never been to Saigon," Joel said.

"Ah, Saigon," Dean said. "The beauty of Paris and the sensibility of the orient."

"Idiot," Mari said.

"I haven't been anywhere," Betsy said.

"You know what?" said Dean. "All of us should get up from this table, cab to JFK, and take the next plane around the world."

"That's your last drink," said Mari.

"I don't know," Joel was musing. "Before, when I said I was thinking."

"About me taking care of myself?" Betsy said.

"Yes." He hesitated and said, "Would you like me to take care of you?"

Betsy sputtered into her wine while Dean and Mari laughed.

Dammit, thought Betsy, she really would like him to take care of her. Say something dummy. Say no way. She said, "How?"

"Getting up from this table, cabbing to JFK, and taking the next plane around the world."

Silence.

Betsy stood.

"Good girl," said Joel, and he stood.

Dean and Mari stood.

"Your coat check?" Joel said.

The three of them were grinning at her but she produced it.

They went. They took the midnight Air France flight to Paris.

Madrid, Cannes, Milan, Rome, and from then on one bedroom for Betsy and Joel instead of two. Dean and

11

Mari flew home from Athens, and Betsy and Joel went on from there. Moscow, Tokyo, Hong Kong and Shanghai. The stays took longer and longer, and so did Joel's almost daily calls to home, to wife as well as the office, but.

But what? She had never been happier. She even liked being taken care of. He would soon be gone and out of her life but she would always have the memories, and at least once in her life, she would have been—what? She laughed. Taken cared of!

Southeast Asia, Australia, South America, everywhere in South America and then Miami and back to New York. Forty-two days. The best days. The best days ever.

They kissed good-bye at JFK, and he was gone and she never saw him again.

Not once. Not even a phone call.

She saw his name in the papers twice, once at a Lincoln Center event and once about some problem with the S.E.C. Otherwise nothing.

Betsy thought about him from time to time as her life went on, a good life, a rich, full one, good not perfect, but no complaints. Two jobs, two husbands, one divorce, the second died, one son with each husband, then a widow with two boys, both boys off to college, alone again, the empty nest syndrome, old age, decent health but not enough to do, too many friends getting sick and dying.

One day the phone rang. "Hello?" she said.

"Hello to you."

No! Impossible! Could it be? Say something clever, you damn fool!

She couldn't think of anything clever so she said, "How long has it been? Thirty years?"

"Twenty-eight years, five months and three days," he said.
"You've prepared this phone call," Betsy said.

"Of course, and thank you for knowing who it was. I always wondered if you would remember."

"Best days of my life."

"Thank you. Even if isn't true, I needed that."

"It is true and I remember you often," Betsy said.

"You always were the sweetest," Joel said.

"Is something wrong? I mean you said you needed that, and there was sort of an implication. Of whatever."

"How about I come over?"

Wow. That was direct. She hesitated. Then, "Sure," she said. "Of course. When?"

"Now? That was a question."

"Sure. Now. You know the address?"

"You going to give me a wrong one?"

She laughed and hung up. As he once had, on her.

He was still handsome. Distinguished. Elegant even.

They stood in her doorway and did not kiss. Or touch. Or anything. They just looked at each other.

"There's something you want to say," she said, knowing there was something wrong, no, something very wrong.

"Yes."

"Say it."

"I don't want to spoil the moment. I mean, standing here, looking at you."

"That's very sweet but say it."

"I'm dying."

"Shit. I'm sorry."

"Thanks."

She was smiling.

He said, "What?"

"Would you like me to take care of you?"

He was emotional. "Yes."

They hugged. "How long do you have?" she said.

"A month, maybe less," he said.

"Let's try to make it forty-two days," she said. "That would be ironic."

"That would be terrific."

It was.

They didn't talk much about his illness, or the trip, or anything else. One day he said, "Do you ever see much of Mari and Dean."

She said, "No, not for years. You?

"Not since they split and Mari closed her agency."

"Do you miss them?" she said. "I do."

He said, "I don't believe in missing."

She decided not to pursue it and a couple of days later he said to her, "Love. What is it? Are we in love?"

She laughed. "Speak to me of love," she said.

"Parlez-moi d'amour."

"Yes. Please. I always loved that song."

Of course he changed the subject.

They got exactly the forty-two days, and she was in the hospital with him, holding his hand, at his last moment.

CHAPTER TWO

Betsy opened the door and entered, saying, "Hello?"

Silence. The bedroom door was closed, meaning that Annie was in the bedroom.

Betsy put her coat in the closet noisily, so Annie would know for sure she was home, if. She smiled because "if" would be nice, as Annie had been down the last couple of weeks. Betsy would sleep on the couch, if, and he was going to spend the night.

Hmm. She did need to shower and the bathroom was off the bedroom. Noises from the bedroom, but not that kind of noise. Betsy opened the fridge, took out a coke and closed the fridge. Quietly. She opened the cupboard, took out a glass, popped the coke can, and was pouring when the bedroom door opened.

Annie came out with a boy. Young, good-looking, not man but boy. "Hi, sweetness," said Annie. "This is Fred. This is my roommate Betsy, Fred."

Betsy said, "Hi." Fred said, "Pleased to meet."

"We're going out for dinner, would you like to come?" said Annie.

"Don't be silly," Betsy said. "I'm going to shower and scramble some eggs."

"Um," Annie hesitated.

"Sure," said Betsy. "I can sleep on the couch."

"Now that's a good roommate!" Fred said.

He was right. Betsy was. Too good, as it happened, as Fred stayed, and stayed for weeks. He was neat, even in the bathroom, he kept his clothes in a small suitcase under Betsy's bed, he made the beds every day and went off to work. Correction, to seek work.

Unfortunately, he hadn't found work. He was out every day looking, and jobs weren't all that plentiful for an architect draftsman, which is what he said he was or, more likely, what he wanted to be. Annie said he was really trying, hard. She and Fred had made a list of local architects, and Fred had sent six his resume, gone to interviews with two, and then sent out six more resumes. It wasn't a bad resume. He had graduated from Michigan and done a grad school year at M.I.T.

But no job and he was still there.

One night in week two, Betsy had dropped off to sleep when she realized that Annie was sitting on the arm of the couch.

"All okay?" said Betsy.

"Yes, yes. Um," said Annie. "Would you like to join us?"

"Wow. For a three?"

Annie nodded.

"Your idea or his?"

"Both," said Annie. "With you every night out here, alone, you know what I mean?"

"I don't do threes, sweetheart, we've discussed it."

"I know, you have this dream man who gets his thrills from your responses, but Fred's here, and he's very good, and he's more than willing."

"No. And I don't mean to be rude, so please tell him thanks, but no thanks. Okay?"

22

"Good night. Sweet Betsy."

Betsy rolled over and tried to go back to sleep. Would the episode make things awkward?

Yes, it did. Sort of. Every time Fred looked at her, she had to wonder what he was looking at, and thinking about, and she had to monitor her own responses which were consistently, and happily, negative. Even so, it was awkward.

It had been six weeks plus and still no job and damn it, she and Annie were splitting the rent and Fred was paying nothing. He did chip in for the groceries, and sometimes he even did the shopping, and he paid for the groceries with his own money once. No, let's be fair, he had paid twice.

But nothing for the rent. Ever.

And Betsy was still sleeping on the living room couch.

"Annie," said Betsy one morning after Fred left. "Whose place is it?"

"Yours and mine. Ours."

"That's what it used to be," Betsy said.

"Sweetheart, really, it still is."

"You and I pay the rent."

"Because it still is."

"But time marches on and he is still here. And paying nothing."

"Because he can't. You know he can't," Annie said.

"How about a third? Something? Less than a third?"

"He has no job. And less than five hundred dollars."

"And when he's totally broke, then what?" said Betsy. "We feed him, too?"

"You want to throw him out? You expect me to throw the poor guy out?"

"Sweetheart, I'm not telling you what to do, but what's the plan? The end game?"

"I don't know," said Annie. "What do you suggest?"

"A reasonable time. All right? Okay?"

"Sure. Let me speak to him."

Maybe Annie spoke to him, and maybe she didn't, but she never told Betsy, and enough was enough.

Betsy told the story to Mort. He laughed.

"Shit," he said. "Enough is enough. Would you like to move in with me again? You should. You really have to."

"That isn't what I had in mind."

"Oh? Isn't it?"

Betsy was suddenly unsure but she said, "No."

"Let's discuss the possible arrangements," Mort said. A lawyer, he wanted things crystal clear. He was the youngest partner in a 200-lawyer firm where she was a paralegal until she worked on a case for him. She had left when the case was over, despite his objections.

"Nobody knows," he had said.

"But they will," she had said. "I want to be out of here before that happens."

He had helped her get a job elsewhere with his glowing

26

recommendations and they had lived together for slightly less than a year. She had left on good if not the best of terms when she and Annie became friends.

"Well?" he said.

All right, the arrangements. He would want her to sleep with him, and that would be okay, no, okay plus, but he was nowhere near the dream man she was searching for, waiting for.

"What?" said Mort, impatiently. "What's the problem. You involved with someone?"

"No."

"Then what? You don't want to sleep with me? You don't have to sleep with me. Look, it's my place, let's not forget, and there's no long term commitment. In fact, there's no commitment. I'm free, and you're free, and there are two beds in the bedroom."

"Yours," she said, smiling.

"You sure? Then let's."

She offered to pay something for the rent, not half, because she couldn't afford half, but she could pay what she was paying with Annie, and she that would be the least that would be fair, but Mort wouldn't take it. He told her to save it for her own place. Sooner or later she would have enough for a place of her own and, to the extent she saved, he would feel less pressure.

"Pressure?" said Betsy.

"Pressure," said Mort. "We're not going to marry or commit long term and sooner or later either you or me, I, will meet someone and need a place of our own, and if it's me, and you're stone cold broke, that would be pressure. So take your rent share and bank it."

"You make it sound like 'stuff it.'"

"I didn't mean it like that. Look, my job is to worry about what can go wrong, and take whatever steps I can to avoid it."

"That's an awful way to go through life," Betsy said.

"A lawyer's life is not a happy one, happy one?"

"Policeman. A policeman's life. Pinafore."

"Did you ever date a policeman?" Mort said.

"No, why?"

"I don't know. I just said it."

He just said it, but she knew what had produced it. He wanted her out there, dating. Because he wanted to be dating, too. They weren't. Not yet, but it was coming.

What to do?

She started leaving work a little early, stopping for a drink at Charley's, and coming home just little bit later than before. She sat at the bar and ordered a gimlet, and waited to see what landed. It never took more than a minute or two. Charley's was a fuck bar, as it was explained to her by an elderly gent, Sheldon, who sat beside her on night number three.

"Men and women both," he said. "I have classified the women. Class One the immediately's. 'Let's' is all you have to say."

"And they say?"

"'Whose place? Yours or mine.'"

"Class Two?"

"The minute or two's. They want to talk for a minute or two, to see what they're getting into. No, I mean the reverse."

She laughed. "I know what you mean. Class Three?"

"The ten's. Want to talk for ten minutes. Class Four, they're the dinner firsts. To see if he can talk, what he likes to talk about, who he talks about, him or her, and finally does he reach for the check."

"Don't women nowadays split the check?"

"No," said Sheldon. "And may I pick up yours? You're a good-looking woman." He reached for it.

She shook her head and said, "That's a new one, asking."

Mort seemed to know but said nothing, so she escalated the

following week and went home for an hour with someone. A handsome Alec someone. His apartment was stunning but he was not. He asked for her phone. She didn't give it to him.

"Working late?" said Mort. Suspicion.

"There's a Friday hearing. I'm checking the plaintiff's brief citations. Do they say what the brief says they say."

"Fun," he said. Seemingly acceptance.

The blonde short haircut at the end of the bar was looking at her, making up his mind. Was he shy? she was wondering.

"Whatcha drinking?" said the hulk beside her. Muscles, and probably thought he was smoothe.

She hesitated. Oh, what the hell. "A gimlet," she told him.

"Know who invented the gimlet?" he said.

She did, but thought he didn't. She looked at him.

"Raymond Chandler," he said, surprising her.

"THE LONG GOODBYE. But let's make this a short one."

He preened, misunderstanding, so she clarified, "Good night. Goodbye."

"Shit. I thought we were scoring."

He left, reluctant, and hooray! Blondie was arriving. He took the hulk's chair. "I couldn't help listening," he said.

She smiled and said nothing.

"Did you see the movie?" he said

"I hated it," she told him. "Elliott Gould while still married to Streisand, directed by Robert Altman from a script having nothing to do with the book, or no script, being Altman. But I did like Sterling Hayden. I always liked Sterling Hayden."

"Wow."

"Did you like Sterling Hayden?"

"I meant wow, you know a lot about movies."

"Thanks."

"Hayden was in the O.S.S. and later in the C.I.A. And a communist."

"How do you to know all that?"

"I must have been told by someone."

"In the C.I.A.?"

"No, I remember who it was. A woman I took to an ASHPHALT JUNGLE rerun!"

She sipped her drink. He ordered his own gimlet, Tanqueray. Pointed to hers. She shook her head. They sat there waiting for his. It arrived. He put two $20 bills on the bar. The bartender's eyebrows rose.

"Both," said Blondie, indicating hers.

She hesitated, then "Thanks," she said.

He grinned. "Elliott," he said. "Please call me Ell."

"Betsy."

"How do you do. What?" She was smiling, shaking her head. He said it again, "What?"

"I come here after work some days, but I never told anyone my name before."

"Maybe if I took you to dinner, you'd tell me your last name and phone number, too?"

"I don't make man-woman deals."

"I would love to take you to dinner. Please?"

Dinner was a ten on a scale of ten. The food was good, Mexican, with a full bar, and it even had their Tanqueray gin, the very gin she preferred, so they each had another gimlet and dipped chips into the sauce. She had taco salad without the tacos and mixed it herself. He had a shrimp ceviche and a shredded beef enchilada, and they talked about her, and places, and things, and their views on the coming election. He seemed to know everyplace and everything and didn't know how he knew what he knew.

As for what he did for a living, that, he apologized, was hard to explain. The firm he worked for called themselves consultants so that was what he supposed you would call him. For whom were they consulting? The government. Several different agencies. Could he possibly be more specific than that? He could, but he shouldn't. And her?

Her. She found herself telling him about the case she was on, more than she should have told him, but he wanted to know the details and he did ask intelligent questions. She came from Westerly, Rhode Island, and Bryn Mawr; she could have gone to Brown but turned it down, too politically correct an institution. He was born in Philadelphia, not the one near Bryn Mawr, guess where? She had no idea. Mississippi, he told her, laughing. College? He had gone to three or four, but principally Northwestern.

They had Mexican coffees, whipped cream and liqueurs. And then?

A few moments of silence.

Ell called for the check.

She produced her credit card.

He laughed. "Don't be ridiculous."

"Please? It's now the custom."

"My father would kick me in the ass."

"Oh. A Mississippi southern gentleman?"

"Hardly. A cop."

"Is he still alive?"

"No. Shot dead in a traffic stop."

"Oh, I'm sorry."

"Mom died when they told her. I came back for the funerals."

"Any brothers or sisters?"

"None. Never set foot in Mississippi again."

The check came and he paid it.

"Thank you," she told him.

"Home?" he said. "May I take you home?"

Well, she thought. That was polite. And also ambiguous. She said nothing, thinking.

Ell said more. "Look, this has been good. Promising. Let's leave it where we are, okay? Here's my card." He produced it. Name and phone number only, but raised print. She ran her thumb over the print.

"I don't have a card," she said.

He handed her another card and a pen. "Please?"

"Sure."

The taxi dropped her off at eleven fifteen. She found herself humming. She put her key in the door but it opened and she found herself looking at one of the most beautiful women she had ever seen, brownish red hair all the way to the roots, and Mort, surprised, proud and pleased.

The woman was talking. "Wow! Good looking, sexy, too!" She was talking about Betsy! "Mort, you didn't say she was stunning!"

Mort did the honors, "Betsy, this is Cecilie. Cecilie, Betsy."

"I can stay!" said Cecilie.

Mort had the decency to be embarrassed. "Betsy?"

Betsy said, "You know I don't do threes."

"You should try it," said Cecilie.

"No, thanks," said Betsy. "Mort, please?"

"Betsy wants to shower and go to sleep," Mort said.

She said, "Okay, damn, pity."

When Mort returned he found Betsy in the second bed. Not yet asleep, drowsy. He perched on the edge of the other bed and said, "Want company?"

"That's not funny."

"So it goes. Good night, sweet Betsy."

She said, "I've found my own place but I don't have enough money."

"You've met someone?"

"I don't know. Maybe."

"I'll help with the rent for six months," Mort said. "Or better, come back to my shop and we'll pay you what you're worth, sufficiently."

"No. Please, Mort. I'm sleepy."

Ell phoned, thankfully. They had dinner, inexpensive and Chinese, but the place had Tanqueray and they switched to martinis.

Betsy said, "Do you spell 'Ell' 'e, l, l' or just the letter, capital 'L'?"

"Why? Are you planning to write me?"

"No, but I think of you as 'L'. One letter, just the capital."

"So be it, darling. Now, tell me. What's been going on with you?"

She told him the whole story.

"That was good of Mort, I suppose," L said. "But given what could have happened, he was only being decent."

"You mean, I could have walked in on them in action."

"Poor Betsy. It keeps on happening."

"But whose place is it, damn it? It's his. What I want, and need, is my own place, and I'm going to have it."

"With Mort's help," L said.

"Any other idea?"

"How about a job with better pay?"

"You could get twice what you're earning now at any one of a number of government agencies." He hesitated. He had more to say. "There's something I should tell you."

"Oh oh. What?"

"Security clearance. You have it."

"What? You put me through security?"

"All the way back to Charley."

"My first boyfriend Charley?" Betsy was incredulous.

"I had to. Two dates and I want more. And please, it took guts to tell you because you're probably offended so before you walk out I apologize."

"Shocked. Stunned. And somewhat offended. Jesus Christ, do you work for the C.I.A?"

"Now I'm disappointed."

"By what? What's the matter with my asking?"

"If I don't, I tell you no, and you don't believe me. If I do, I tell you no, and I have lied to you, and I don't want to lie to you, ever, so it's a heads I lose, tails I lose, that kind of question."

Betsy laughed. "Now I apologize."

"Want to work for the agency at double your present salary?"

"You're too much, and this is much too fast."

"I'll tell you what isn't," L said. "Tell human resources where you work that you love it there but you can go elsewhere at double what they're paying you. If you're as good as I think you are, and the people who were asked there think you are, you'll get a significant increase in salary."

"You're serious? About the job and pay? I wouldn't want to be lying."

"So try me. Get yourself fired."

She laughed.

They went to his place. Two bedrooms, the twentieth floor, a view of the river, beautifully decorated. She smiled. "Some woman did this."

"A decorator not a date. I'll give you her name, if you want, call her."

"I haven't got my raise yet."

"Want to move in here?"

"It's your place. I want, I need, my own place. I'm never going to live with a man again unless we are married."

Afterwards she decided that she had had a full hour of consecutive orgasms, one right after another, it was all a blur, or had it been one continuous orgasm lasting an hour? It was the best sex she had ever had and she had at last found a dream man whose pleasure came from pleasing her, and he did, really, wow, did he ever, more and more, over and over.

"I would like to spend the night," she said. "If that's all right with you?"

L laughed.

"You must own all your women."

"There aren't any other women."

"But there have been, lots of them."

"I don't remember anyone."

"That's sweet," she said to him.

"I try," he said. "I keep trying."

She got the raise and it was more than enough. Mort congratulated her and said, "Who is he and what does he do and do I get to meet him?"

She ducked the questions.

The relationship with L was explosive, or it would have been if it were a short term fling but it wasn't just a fling. It went on and on, week after week, month after month, and survived two of his three-week trips abroad. Abroad or somewhere.

She asked where and he told her London. And grinned.

"Don't get killed," she said.

"I'll do my best," he said.

She even liked being alone and missing him. She got a couple of calls from old men friends but didn't call back either of them. She had dinner with Mort several times L was away without a flicker of problem.

The first year passed and they took a cruise and a Caribbean vacation.

"Can it last?" she said. "Does it ever last?"

"Seems to me we're doing fine," L said. "I don't see the problem. Want to marry?"

"And give up a place of my own? And share it with someone?"

She received two office promotions and became the senior paralegal for the primary rainmaker in the firm. She had money for the first time in her life, and phoned L's decorator woman, who redid her apartment top to bottom. She loved it, and so did L. Her place. Her own place.

"My place or yours," they loved to play.

And once or twice a week, "To each his own."

One of those nights someone knocked on her door.

That was strange. No buzzer. Knocking. She was alone, and appropriately cautious. At the door, she said, "Who is it?"

"Guess."

"I can't."

It said, "Damn, that's disappointing. Don't you have a chain, or a lock with an arm? Hey, you have a peephole! Peep through the hole!"

She did. Cautiously. Could it be? Yes! It was Charley!

"Charley!" She unlocked the door. It was Charley. Grinning.

49

They hugged and kissed and she let him in and said, "What in the world are you doing here? You, who swore you'd never come here! You! Small town Charley! Want a drink?"

"Got a beer?"

"Of course."

She went to fetch it. He followed her. She handed him a Bud and a tall glass. He sat at the table and poured it.

"No jobs at home. Got a good one here. In hospital services."

"Great."

"Good to see you again. As always you look terrific."

"And?"

"I need a place to stay for the next two weeks. I get my first pay check on the first of the month and until them I'm totally broke. Credit cards completely maxed out, a hundred and a half in my pocket."

"I'll have to ask," she said.

"You're involved, I assume."

"Oh, yes, very."

"How much would it cost for a hotel? For two weeks?"

"I don't know. I could lend you the money."

"And take me to dinner once or twice?"

She was already phoning.

L answered on first ring. "Hi!"

"Hi, good evening. What kind of a day did you have today?"

Silence. Then "You never ask me that."

"I have a visitor and I feel clumsy."

L laughed. "A man? Who?"

51

"Charley?"

"Charley who? Not your first Charley?"

Betsy felt herself blushing. "Yes. He's broke, but has a job, a good one, but he doesn't get paid until the first of the month. I could lend him a couple of thousand."

"Fine," said L. "It's your money, lend it to him. Do you need to borrow some from me?"

"No, I have enough."

"Oh, I see. You want to put him up."

"Would you mind if I did?"

"Remember Mort and Annie?"

"Yes. But."

"Sweetheart, tell me about the but. No, don't squirm, don't tell me. If you want to put him up, of course put him up. If you want to sleep with him, don't tell me. Okay?"

"You know I wouldn't and I resent the implication."

"Don't. And tell me or don't, it's up to you."

"Can we all have dinner tomorrow night?"

L laughed. "You pick the restaurant."

"How about. . ." she hesitated.

"Your place, darling? Your very own place?"

She said, "I'll pick the restaurant."

She did. It was unexpectedly pleasant, and the three of them had dinner a second time the following week. Betsy had dinner with Charley in restaurants twice, in her place, once, and spent both weekends and Mondays at L's.

On Wednesday, the second day of the month, Charley moved into a hotel after repaying her five hundred dollar pocket money advance, and showering her with endless thanks, not only for her but for L, too, for being kind and understanding.

L phoned her at her office.

"Good morning!"

"He's gone," Betsy said. "With much appreciation. For both of us, you, too."

"That's good. Decent."

"And he repaid my five hundred. Have you seen the new hundred dollar bills?"

"The ATMs downstairs dispense them. Dinner?"

"Of course."

"You pick the place."

She picked the Mexican restaurant of their first date.

They were seated at the very same table, which was fun, and L took over with a big grin, ordering Tanqueray gimlets for each of them, chips and sauce, taco salad without the tacos which Betsy could mix herself, and a shrimp ceviche and shredded beef enchilada for him.

"My goodness," she said. "You remembered every little thing."

"The curse of a photographic memory."

The gimlets arrived. She dipped a chip.

"Let's try it together," L said. "Live together. We almost do."

"You know my opinion. Position."

"Yes. Let's live together," he said.

She swallowed the chip. Looked at him. Said, "Is that a proposal or a proposition?"

"Both."

She sipped her gimlet. He was grinning. Son of a bitch was always grinning. "I'd appreciate something more formal," she said.

"Sure," he said. "Will you marry me?"

"Knees?"

"You want me on my knees?"

"Not yet. There's something you should know."

"Oh oh. I probably do know."

"I want to tell you anyhow."

"Actually," he said, "I wish you wouldn't."

"I slept with him."

Silence. She waited.

56

He said, "Did you like it?"

"Of course I did. He was good, better than he used to be. Not in the same league as you, of course, but what the hell, nobody is."

"Okay. And now that we've got that out of the way, I forgive you for it and for telling me, but you haven't answered the question."

"Knees?" He started to rise.

"Not in public. A kiss will do."

L rose, circled the table, and kissed her. Tenderly. Her eyes teared. She said, "Yes."

The couple at the next table applauded.

L and Betsy said, "Thanks."

Betsy said, "I wish you would ask for the check."

"Without waiting for dinner?"

"Yes."

L produced his credit card and waved it at the waiter, who approached and took it. L said, "Sorry, but we have to leave now. Whatever you charge, it's all okay, including the usual twenty percent." The waiter left.

L grinned that damn grin and said, "Whose place? Mine or yours?"

"Mine is spoiled now. Yours is yours. How about a place that's ours?"

"We can look for one this weekend."

"Great."

The waiter returned with the bill. L signed it and pocketed his credit card.

"Something else we have to discuss," Betsy said.

"Yes. If, how many and when," he said. "It's exactly the same as "Whose place?"

"In what way?"

"Children. You decide."

"It's a mutual decision," Betsy said.

"No," he said. "No, it isn't. You decide. You're the woman."

"It should be mutual," she said again.

"Decide," he said. "You're my woman."

CHAPTER THREE

Betsy was in the front garden picking roses for the kitchen table when she became aware of the Cadillac out on the street. Black. Moving slowly. Checking the numbers probably.
It stopped at her mailbox. Her heart sank. Oh, no.

Two men got out. Sixty, judging by the wispy remaining hair, white shirt, striped tie, three-button dark gray herringbone suit. Nowadays no one wears three-button suits. They don't even sell them anymore. The other one was younger, probably in his thirties. Short hair, no tie, a blue shirt. Navy blue suit. A briefcase. Black leather, expensive.

Betsy took a deep breath. She went to meet them and spoke first. "Is he dead?"

They nodded. Murmured, "Sorry".
Short hair said, "Condolences."

She took a deep breath. "Pain?
Suffering?"

Sixty said, "No. Quick. One moment
there, next moment gone."

"Sounds like an explosion," Betsy
said.

No response. Details classified?

Then, "I'm Arthur," said Sixty.

"Bob," said short hair.

"A and B," said Betsy. "Here about
L. Well? What? Oh, you have some
papers?" She was looking at the
briefcase.

Bob said, "Yes."

"Let's go in. I'll get coffee."

She entered the house.

They followed.

Vilma was holding Ernie by the kitchen door.

"Take Ernie out in the carriage, please," said Betsy.

Vilma nodded, turned, went back through the kitchen and out the garage door.

They followed into the kitchen. Betsy put the roses on the counter. She opened the cupboard up above, to the right of the sink, and took out three mugs for coffee. "Black or something in it? And please sit."

They sat. Arthur wanted black. Bob wanted two sugars. Artificial. Please.

Betsy poured theirs and took her own black. She put theirs on the table, then hers and started to sit. Changed her mind. Fetched Jack Daniels from the liquor cupboard.

Carefully poured a large shot in her cup. Sat. Sipped. Waited.

"The boy is three?" said Bob.

"You must know he is."

"Sorry."

Arthur lifted his mug. "To Elliott."

"L," she said.

They drank.

She gestured at the briefcase, said, "All right. What's in the papers?"

Bob fumbled in the briefcase, took out the papers.

Arthur said, "You and Elliott, you were very close?"

"That's what it says in his Agency file?"

"Probably. That's what he told me."

"And you can't understand my lack of response? You think I'm oddly unemotional?"

"Yes. I don't understand it."

"I've been rehearsing this moment for years and years. No tears, no hysterics, matter of fact. Dignified, if I could manage. L laughed at me when we rehearsed it, but after Ernie I worried more and more that this day would come sooner or later."

Arthur said, "Beau Geste, stout fella."

Bob said, "Gary Cooper."

"Ray Milland, Robert Preston, Brian Donlevy. L loved that movie," said Betsy.

Bob put papers before her.

She blinked, trying to focus. Still no tears. "For me to sign?" she said.

Arthur said, "Yes, dear, but you ought to see a lawyer."

"I don't know who. I don't want to involve my firm."

"We have a list," said Bob, and handed it to her.

"Thanks," she said.

"Use my name. I know them all. Personally."

"Bob?"

"Say it was someone named Bob who said he was from the Agency."

Arthur said, "In summary, you're the sole insurance beneficiary, and there's a substantial bonus in addition to that, given what he was doing, when."

"And if you ever need help," said Bob, "Call me. Help of any kind. Regular or irregular." He handed her a card. Just a telephone number. "And I'm not hitting on you. I'm a married man. Living in D.C. Happily. Helping you would be the very least I could do. He trained me. Elliott trained me." His voice wavered. Tearful.

Arthur said, "Please go wait in the car."

Bob stood, took his briefcase and went out the door. Betsy called after him, "Thank you!"

Arthur gestured toward the papers on the table. "Take a look. Ask whatever occurs to you."

"I'd like to have a funeral. When will he, I mean the body--."

She swallowed. Stopped.

"No body, but you can have a funeral. Or a memorial service. Some do. Whatever. Call me if you don't mind some of us there. Elliott had really close friends. He was very well-regarded."

"Thanks. That's good to know. But no, I don't think so. Explaining to people--." Her voice broke again.

"I see. So no. Anything else you want to ask?"

"Yes."

"What?"

"Would you please leave now. I'm going upstairs with the bottle."

She decided no body, no funeral. Too much to explain, too awkward. And no memorial.

The phone calls started three days later, nevertheless, after the TIMES printed a short obit. L had been a consultant for the Department of State specializing in international conflict. He was survived by his long term companion and their son, names withheld at their request.

Betsy didn't know the TIMES would do that and she never read obits. She hadn't read L's till the phone calls. She read it then several times. Shouldn't someone have spoken to her? No, it was for L, not for her.

She phoned McAlister, the firm rainmaker for whom she worked, and arranged to take the rest of the week off. "To sulk," was the way she put it.

"Don't do that to yourself, you're in mourning, take all the time you feel you need, and don't feel any pressure. Come back when you feel like it, not before."

Tears. She couldn't help it.

She went back to work a week later. She started working Saturday mornings. McAlister found out and came to see her.

"What are you doing here Saturdays?"

"You're here."

"Yes, but nobody else is."

"I like it. The work. And being alone here."

"What about the boy?"

"He plays with friends, and I'm always home in the afternoon."

Silence.

She said, "There's something else you want to say."

He said, "I'm thinking."

"Let me guess. 'When you're ready, and not before, there's someone I think you ought to meet?'"

"Since it's clear that you can read my mind, why don't you take over my correspondence."

She laughed. "A year," she said. "I'm going to wait a year. A proper period of mourning."

69

"Why? Is that some religious thing?"

"No," she said. "It's my thing. Do you think I'm wrong? I'll take that from you."

"That's the nicest thing anyone has said to me for a long long time." He took out his handkerchief. "I'd better leave you alone now."

He left.

She kept working.

She kept a list. Who called, the date they called, the name of the man prospect. Eventually there were a dozen prospects, several recommended multiple times.

She never answered a prospect call and small dinner parties at the homes of good friends were the only places she ever met them. She made a record of the names, times and places and those with the sense not to phone.

McAlister took her to dinner every other week, and included his wife often. Irene. She was an editor. Betsy liked her. He tried to pay for the sitter on dinner nights but Betsy wouldn't hear of it. She really liked them and the dinners.

She had lunch with girlfriends, never men. No concerts, theatre or movies, no benefits, or occasions, or parties of more than a dozen.

A year passed.

Ernie was now in play school. She went with him the first day. No tears from that kid, L's son. Another stout fella. She was proud of him. Her tears started. He hugged her. At that she really cried. He was devastated, tried to reassure her.

She started accepting invitations. A man a month. A new man. Two dates maximum. The moment she heard "Whose place?" she laughed. They invariably found the laugh puzzling and asked for an explanation.

"I don't know you well enough," she always said.

"I'd like to know you better," they always said.

"No, thanks" was usually sufficient.

Two called again anyhow. She had a speech for them. "Look, you're a very nice man but I'm not the woman you're looking for."

"Pity," was the response both times, but they got the message and stopped calling.

Ernie was now in kindergarten. She went with him the first day although he told her she needn't. She said she wanted to. He told her it would embarrass him.

"In kindergarten for Chrissake!"

"You swore, Mom."

"I'm entitled to take my son to school!"

He muttered, but agreed, reluctantly.

She went.

He kissed her goodbye at the school entrance and ran, not walked, away through the school door.

Tears again.

Mort appeared in her office the following week. She hadn't heard from him since his condolence call and hadn't seen him for what seemed like ten full years. Was it really ten?

No, it wasn't.

Cheek kisses, and "To what do I owe the honor?" she said.

He was carrying a manila folder and looked about. "Do you mind if I close the door?" He closed it without waiting for an answer. Sat. Smiled.

She smiled.

He said, "Sweetheart, you are thirty-three years old. One child. One marriage."

She said, "Sort of."

"I forgot. You and L never married?"

He waited and she didn't answer.

He went on. "Widowed. Financially secure on your own now. Don't need to work but you do, here, and you do because you love it and they love you. Independent. Self-supporting. A wonderful mother to her little boy."

"How would you know that?"

74

"Everyone says. All your friends. Annie. Even Dean and Mari."

"So?"

"There are dozens and dozens of men in this town dreaming of meeting a woman like you, good men, intelligent, reliable, good catches as my mother would say. I myself know at least a dozen men. You have dated half a dozen of them but nobody seems to make the cut."

She waited.

He continued on. "You like sex. You know I know you do. And yet you've been celibate for what? Years?"

"How would you know that?"

"Men talk. Nearly all men. Some of those you've dated. Some of them have even asked me if you're gay, or frigid."

Betsy said, "If you're selling, and you seem to be, you're not coming across."

"I am thirty-seven, no kids, one divorce. Money in the bank and real estate. Worth many times what I hoped to be. Sexually adequate."

"Adequate plus."

"Not in the same league as L."

"No."

"Sweetheart, I think you should marry me."

She couldn't help giggling.

"What's so funny?"

"The proposals I get. This one sounds like a business deal."

"I'm a lawyer. That's what I do. Here." He handed her the manila folder.

"What's this?" she said.

"Financial statement. Profit and loss. Partnership agreement. Tax returns. Divorce settlement."

"Oh, my. Wow. You're serious. You're not kidding."

"You're repeating yourself."

"What kind of marriage? You know what I mean."

"Traditional. Exclusive. Commitment. Sickness and health. Till death. Okay?"

"I get to work as long as I want?"

"Agreed."

"And the little thing you forgot to say?"

He grinned. "You know me well."

"Well?"

"One child. I want a son."

"Not a girl? That's fifty fifty."

"Not any more. I want a son. So?"

"I don't know what to say."

"I do. You have three choices," he said. "Fuck off, yes, or I'll think about it. Look, we lived together once. For nearly a year. It was good. We talked. Both of us almost liked it. True?"

"True."

"So what do you say?" he said.

Pause.

"You know what?" she said. "I'm going to surprise you."

"Well?"

She smiled. "I'll think about it."

She did. And made a suggestion, cautiously. "Let's date for a while, not yet exclusively."

He agreed, and they did.

She spent the night at his place. Twice.

She twice dated others. Mort knew. She made sure he knew. She had to. Sandy was one of his friends. "What can I say?" he said. "I hope you had a good time."

She had and she hadn't. No, she had. Sort of. She told him.

He shrugged, took it without comment.

McAlister spoke to her. "You've been seeing Mort."

"Is that a question?"

"No. On the contrary. Good man. Very different from what he was before. And nothing like what you had before."

She smiled. "Do we have your blessing?"

"My blessing is inappropriate."

"Yes, it is. I think it is."

"Dear, you are thirty-six. Time flies. Does he want children? I hope you don't mind my asking."

"No, and he does. He wants a son."

"How old is Ernie now, six? How would he feel about it? He's always been an only child."

"A brother would be good for him."

"He'd be seven, eight years older. Oh, and one other thing. There's always one thing more."

"Yes?"

"This time, if you do it, marriage, please. For Ernie, and Irene and me."

"Sure. Would you like to be there?"

They would and they were.

She had butterflies the night before. She had married before for passion, love, the rich feeling of total commitment, the emotional envelopment of this was it, the big love of her lifetime, and what in hell was she about to do? She liked Mort, she was comfortable with him, she was always happy to see him, he made her laugh, she liked talking to him, she liked being with him and not even talking to him, but. But. But what? Her toes didn't tingle? That was childish? Or was it truly once in a lifetime?

On the other hand, she was pregnant. Damn fool careless. Mort didn't know. It would be easy to what, terminate? What was it, a boy or a girl? Wasn't it too soon to tell? Get married, or she'd never know. It was Sandy's and it wasn't Mort's and that was a problem.

She decided to get married anyhow.

She was smiling when the priest said, "Husband and wife." Everyone thought she was happy and maybe she was but the joke was on everyone, no one knew, and nobody would ever know the reason she got married. One of the reasons. To give Ernie a sibling. She would always love Ernie more anyway. That was something she couldn't help. Ernie was L. He was L's and hers. And he wanted, needed, a sibling.

The McAlisters were there, and Annie, Dean and Mari, two couples from the office, the next door neighbors, her childhood sweetheart, Charley, his wife, Mort's mother, his father was dead, his best man and best friend, Sandy, his wife, two other Mort friends, one with a wife, and a stranger in the back of the church, no, it was Bob of A and B, what the hell was he doing here?

Everybody was kissing her. She was
kissing Ernie. She promised herself,
if Ernie turned out to like Gregory, it
was a boy and Mort had named him
Gregory, then someday she would
tell her secret to somebody.
Probably Ernie. Certainly someone.

Secrets were no damned fun unless
you could tell someone.

Time passed quickly. Then even
more quickly.

She sold her place and he sold his.
They got a large apartment in the
city and a three-bedroom place in
Sag Harbor. They bought them both
together, half her money and half
his, and took title to both together.
They didn't have a prenup and didn't
want a breakup agreement now.

One day she wasn't young any more.
She was forty!

They had a party.

Ernie got into Exeter. He had applied on his own and they had let him apply as there was no way he was going to get in there, his teachers gave him great recommendations but his grades weren't really good enough, he had taken the SSAT with a bad cold and no preparation and gotten a fair plus score, and they really didn't know anyone, or so she thought until she got a message on her answering machine: "Tell Ernie congratulations from his father's friends."

Bob? Arthur? Someone.

Did they want him to go? She didn't. It wasn't the money, which was God-awful, but they had enough, actually she did have enough money all by herself but Mort was insisting on helping.

Mort insisted Ernie had to go. It was something the kid had accomplished all by himself and they had no right to prevent him. And no, it was not so she could devote herself to Gregory, she was a marvelous mother to Gregory, everything he could ever wish for, and everything Mort would wish, and don't dare suggest that was his reason.

Strange for him to say a thing like that. It would never have occurred to her.

They drove Ernie to Exeter and dropped him off and she couldn't seem to stop crying on the way home. She didn't stop until they hit Route 495 and started circling Boston.

"Thinking of L?" said Mort. Gently.

No, she hadn't been thinking of L. She never thought of L any more. At that thought, she started crying again. She stopped at the Massachusetts Turnpike Entrance.

Mort said, "I'll do the same if Greg gets in."

At that moment, for the first time, she somehow knew that Greg wouldn't. He was a good kid and plenty smart enough but Ernie seemed to have something. Like L had had something.

Mort turned 50 and they had another party.

Betsy wanted to give him a present. Something special. Expensive but not ridiculous. She said, "Is there anything you'd really like to have?"

"A red sportscar and a mistress," Mort said, and added, flippantly, "I'm fifty and that's what fifty-year-old men want."

"Actually, they want that at forty," she said. "Please? I want to get you something nice."

"You know what? I'll be skiing Aspen this year. Europe is all Moslem nowadays. How about new skis, new poles, new boots? They'll cost you two thousand?"

"Sure." She kissed him. "Perfect."

He returned the kiss. A bit hard, his kiss. He turned away.

Betsy thought about it. A red sportscar and a mistress and skiing was the very next thought. She started to put the dots together and decided to forget it.

But she couldn't.

Mort had always loved skiing. He had gone skiing in Europe for ten days every year, Val d'Isere and Kitzbuhl for many years, and Gstaad each of the last three years. Betsy didn't ski and refused to try so Mort went with friends every year, Dean and Mari most years, other friends occasionally, Sandy the last couple of years. Sandy had divorced again. Would Mort be going to Aspen with Sandy?

At dinner last night, she said, "What about Dean and Mari this year?"

"What about them?"

"Aspen. You're going to Aspen."

"Oh," said Mort. "Good idea." He looked at his watch. "After dinner, I'll have to call them."

He didn't.

She was nearly asleep when she heard him say, "Dammit, I forgot to call Dean and Mari. In the morning, I'll call them."

He did. But the dates didn't work for them.

Mort and Sandy went to Aspen.

It was like what she said about doctors. If you go looking for trouble hard enough, sooner or later you'll find it. Betsy pushed the suspicions out of her head. At least she tried to do it.

She was comfortable, happy from time to time, she loved the boys and Mort, too, in the case of Mort, not what she had had before, but better than she had expected, or indeed had any right to expect, given the quality of her total commitment previously. Was Mort as happy as she was? She always thought he was. God knows she had kept up her end of the deal, and that's what it was, a marriage deal, and that was the trouble, that's all that it was, a deal not a total marriage. She certainly knew the difference. She had had a total marriage.

So what if he were looking for spice elsewhere? Men did. Many men did. Maybe even most men did. At least Mort held it down to a week and did it out of town and far away.

Or did he?

What if it was going on here, and often, or maybe even all the time?

Put it out of your head, darling.

No, no, she must be wrong. The sex was as good as it ever had been and he was avid, after it all the time.

Shut your head off, Betsy darling.

She did and time marched on and on.

Her nest was now empty. Greg had gone off to Choate Rosemary Hall, "and his exposure to the adolescent drug culture," Ernie sniped. Ernie was now at Harvard. The boys got along magnificently but she hadn't told the secret to Ernie yet. He was majoring in math and computer science and was preparing to write some sort of thesis. He had tried to tell her about it but she didn't know what any of the words meant.

Thank God she had her job and the office!

But McAlister was talking about retirement and that would be a blow to her. Who else would she be willing to para for?

Three more pretty good years passed and then Mort went skiing again, this time thank goodness with Dean and Mari. Not in January as in most years, but in March, much later.

Betsy met Lois Masters at Trader Joe's. She had never really like Lois but greeted her cheerfully with, "Hey! You look great! Where did you get the tan? Florida?"

"Aspen," said Lois. "We just got back. Spring skiing, lots of sun. Terrific. Saw Mort."

"He'll be back Saturday. I'm shopping here for him today. He really loves the cheddar. Won't let me buy it elsewhere."

"We stayed at Little Nell, too. Saw him in the dining room. With Dean and Mari and whatshername, you know, Doris. Miller. You met her at Mari's."

"The editor."

"Yes. That's the one."

"A really good skier."

That was it. That was all it took. Betsy added two and two and got six. And Dean and Mari were in on it! Shit! That would hurt. Really hurt. Better not think about it.

What should she do about it?

Mort liked her to pick him up at the airport. It was raining hard so she texted "No way."

He didn't get home until half past eight. They greeted. Kissed. A light mouth kiss, not just a cheek kiss. "Want to shower before dinner?" she said.

"You bet. Planes are filthy. First class is still filthy. I'm going to drop my clothes on the floor. Could you put them in the washer?"

She said, "No, but you can."

He showered and paid no attention.

The table was set. She got the wine while she heard him dressing. She poured each of them a glass of the Walmart red, the six dollar Walmart red, but left the bottle in the wine cupboard. They had tried it once before and Betsy had liked it but Mort had sneered. Mort was a big wine snob. Probably a fake wine snob. A fake, a faker at lots of things. Let's see if he recognized it.

She was sitting. He kissed the top of her head and sat. "Pasta bolognese! Great!" He served himself a copious portion, passed it to her and sipped his wine.

"Mm! Really good! What is it?"

"Bordeaux. Prairie Cross. Vintage 2000."

"A great year! Croix de Prairie! I've been there. There's a chateau with the name Croix de Prairie. Have you ever been there?"

"No. I've never been in Aspen either."

"Oh?" He wasn't stupid. He put his fork down. "Let's have it."

"Doris Miller."

"Lois Masters. She told you. I knew she would as soon as I saw her. What happened? She phoned, or you met someplace? You and she never hit it off."

"Who? Masters or Miller?"

"Masters," he said. "Miller you hardly know. You met her only once, she liked you."

"And apparently liked you, too."

"How much do you want to know?"

"How much?" she said. "All of it."

He played with his fork. Sighed. Pathetic shit. She hardly listened as he said, "Six months. Once or twice a week. We never traveled. Before Aspen, I mean. That's the first time."

"Well, that's something, I suppose, only one trip together. How often did you leave a bed with her, come merrily home and pork me?"

"You never knew, so what did it matter?"

"I never even suspected."

"So?"

"That's not completely true. It's all been going flat for years, although not in the bed, you have me there. No, correction, had me there."

"Past tense, meaning finis?"

"Hotel. Call one and get out of here."

"Oh, come on, just a minute!"

"Big stud Mort, the two-woman man, how many times in a single night?"

"I will not leave here."

"You will not spend the night in bed with me. And don't try. I don't recommend it."

He wouldn't leave. He didn't take her seriously. He decided to wait her out. He told her that. "I humbly apologize. I promise to break it off quick. I'll never never do it again."

At that she realized something she had not wanted to face, but now she had to face it. "How many others before her? And when did it start?"

He hesitated and that was all it took. She said, "Too many to count and you don't remember?"

"I kept planning to talk it out with you, I never thought you'd be jealous."

"Jealous? Who is jealous?" she said. "I'm not at all jealous. We had an agreement. It was specific. You broke it. And I find I don't like you any more."

"That's pretty harsh," he said.

"McAlister has drawn the papers. Tell me, where do want them served? Here or the office?"

"I'm better than McAlister. You better get some other."

"All I want is your half of the houses. Both. The apartment here, the house in Sag Harbor."

"Sweetheart, I'll see you in hell first. We'll let the probate judge decide it."

"And you know all the judges?"

He smiled. Smirked.

"He does," McAlister told her.

"I don't want it to go to court. Both of the boys would be there, and it could get dirty, I don't know how, but don't underestimate what he might do. I'm clean, which you were too polite to ask. Faithful. Committed."

"And any testimony to the contrary would be false?"

"Yes."

"Unfortunately he has some."

"Who?"

"I don't know. Some friend he says. I haven't filed interrogatories, you don't want it on the record."

"No. Damn. That's pretty discouraging."

"Mort is a scumbag. We know he is."

Long pause. He smiled.

"What?" she said.

"It doesn't matter. Mort will acquiesce."

"No, he won't. You don't know him. He told me he'll see me in hell first."

"Tomorrow he'll sign the papers. I sent them over this afternoon. Oh, and he's going to a hotel tonight."

"What is it you're not telling me?"

"What I don't want to tell you. Just that you seem to have forgotten who you are. Ten o'clock tomorrow morning, conference room in his office."

At ten o'clock the following morning, Betsy and McAlister went to Mort's office. Mort was waiting in a conference room with two other lawyers. Partners?

Nobody said a word in greeting. Everyone but Mort simply nodded.

They sat.

Mort held a pen in his hand. He said, "You really want me to sign this?"

Betsy started to answer but McAlister stopped her. He said, "Yes."

"I'm going to tell the bitch what happened," Mort said.

Both of his partners protested. "Don't!" and "Don't be a fool!" they said.

Mort said, "The taxi that picked me up last night took me to the Park Plaza. I protested when he took the first wrong turn, then I tried the door.

I couldn't upon the door. We turn the corner at 61st and this guy gets in. 'Hi,' he says. 'I'm your conscience. You're going to do the right thing.'"

"'Which is what?' I said."

"You're going to sign the papers tomorrow morning at ten o'clock in the conference room at your office."

"I said, 'I'll see you in hell first.'"

"He says, 'Let me tell you what hell is. Hell is a bad accident and six months in the hospital and limping thereafter forever. Every client you have leaves you. Every case you have goes sour and your partners decide you're the kiss of death. And then you have another accident and again you're in the hospital. But none of that needs to happen if you sign the papers.'"

McAlister said, "We know nothing whatsoever about this. She has no idea what you're talking about."

Betsy said, "What is this? I don't get it. The Russians or the Mafia? I don't know any Russians or Mafia."

"You really are stupid," Mort said.

"Mort," she said, "don't sign it."

McAlister sighed.

Betsy went on, "If you think I had anything to do with it, or anything like that, please don't sign the papers."

Mort looked at her. He signed the papers. He pushed them across the table for her to sign.

McAlister gave her his pen.

"Mort, shut up," one of his partners said as Betsy was signing the papers and McAlister was gathering them up.

"L," said Mort. "Elliott."

Betsy looked at him.

Both of Mort's partners groaned.

Betsy said, "Mort, there's someone I could call. A telephone number to call, 'if'. Mort, to me this is an 'if'".

"The man in the taxi at 61st?" He laughed, a bitter laugh. "No, dear, it's done, forget it."

McAlister said one thing later. "He did the right thing. It was the only right thing. So forget it and never bring it up again."

She didn't.

Neither did McAlister.

It was B, she decided. Maybe she should thank him? No, that would make a record and he would think she was stupid.

She had never thought of calling him, and maybe that had been stupid.

Betsy and Mort told the boys together. The boys said they were sorry. What else could they say.

Later she told Ernie the secret.

He laughed. What a sweet kid. He said, "Greg's my brother. I'll never tell him."

CHAPTER FOUR

One day she was 50, and the next day she was 55.

Nobody but McAlister and the boys wished her Happy Birthday, but life was good and she kept busy. McAlister was doing acquisitions and mergers, and she and her team, which was now her own team, reviewed all the contracts and all the leases. She spent evenings and weekend days comfortably at home, streaming, and of course she had theatre, ballet and music and theatre showings of movie oldies but goodies.

She had a list of friends, nearly all women friends, with whom she had lunch at least once a month, and kept a record of the dates she saw them. She was regularly invited to parties as the much needed single woman, and the eligible divorces and widowers kept relentlessly calling.

She accepted dinner invitations at least a month apart and insisted on going home alone in limousines or taxis.

The McAlisters took her to dinner once a month, then eventually once in six weeks, then in unpredictable nows and thens. He talked of retiring and worked part-time and wow! would she ever miss him.

She sold the house in Sag Harbor when the boys begged off after a summer week and then made excuses about even summer weekends.

The boys were great, however, both of them.

Ernie did a graduate year at M.I.T., two years at the Harvard Business School, two years at Bain, and was now a professor at M.I.T. teaching courses and doing research and consulting in some sort of abstruse computer science beyond her understanding.

Greg had gone to Yale Law and was now a hot-shot associate at a powerhouse New York trial firm.

Neither of the boys had married, although Ernie had had long term relationships with two different women, and Betsy had liked both of them. Liked, admired, and wanted as daughters-in-law, but the first had accepted a London bank job, and the present incumbent, Annamarie, a VP of a Boston advertising firm, was a live-in but had said to Betsy, "Nobody gets married any more unless they want children, and not even then, sometimes."

Betsy knew better than to question.

Greg was a bit of a problem. He never dated the same girl more than twice. "Three dates and they want a relationship," he said. Indeed, he said it often.

She said, "So?"

"I'm refining my sex technique."

"Stop that, I'm your mother."

"Did you realize that four girls a week, two hundred a year, and in five years I will have had a thousand women?"

"You're sick," she said, "and you only told me that because I'd find it irritating!"

"You know what?" Greg said, escalating. "I'm the local golden one-night stand. Women call me all the time. Women tell other women."

"Greg, there's a doctor I wish you'd see."

He kissed her and fled, laughing.

Betsy found herself telling Mari over lunch.

Mari laughed also. "This is a sex-crazed community. It has been since the sixties." Mari hesitated, thinking of something. Wanting to say something.

"I guess it swept past me," Betsy said.

"The latest fashion is ladies."

"Which?"

Mari smiled. "Ladies with ladies."

"Gays?"

"No, dear, not gays, but ladies with ladies."

"Including you?" said Betsy.

"Yup."

"Does Dean know?"

"And approves," Mari said. "He likes to watch."

"You do threes?" Betsy said.

"Heavens, no!" Mari said. "I wouldn't want to watch him fucking other women."

"Oh, my, this is too much for me."

"No, it isn't," said Mari. "Look, you're pretty. Very. Still. You must know I've always thought you were. I would love to service you."

"Service me. And then vice versa."

"Not unless you wanted to."

Betsy took a deep breath and said, "You're trying to seduce me."

"Of course. And I'm succeeding."

"No, you're not."

"No?"

"I don't mean to offend," said Betsy. "But the thought of another woman, even one I know and like, even you, ugh, no way, that's not me."

"All right," said Mari. "Sorry." And smiled. "No problem."

It really shook Betsy.

The biggest merger ever was consuming her, seven days a week for the next six weeks. McAlister's largest fee ever, stories in the press every day, she would have liked to talk about it, but she couldn't, of course, that would be against the law, and she would have liked to invest, but that was also illegal.

It closed, and McAlister retired.

Shit.

They assigned her to Newbury. She rather liked Newbury, but Newbury was not McAlister; he never had been and never would be.

Betsy cleaned her desk. Really. It was empty. Her desk had never been clean for years. She looked up.

There was a man in the doorway. Grinning. She said, "Can I help you?"

He said, "You don't remember me?"

She tried. Got it! "Bob?"

He smiled and sat. "Actually, it should be Bill. My first names are William Robert."

"Still B to me. Look, I didn't phone to thank you because I didn't want to make a record. I thought that would be stupid."

"I would have said I didn't know what you were talking about."

"Of course you would. So here we are. Thanks. And good to see you." She smiled.

He paused. Said, "My wife died."

"Oh. I'm sorry," said Betsy.

"Thanks."

Another pause and Betsy said, "And that covers everything?"

"Actually, really."

"Oh. Me divorced, you widower?"

"Yes, and your fairy godfather, but definitely not a fairy."

She laughed.

He said, "What's so funny?"

"The third time this has happened to me, and at this point I always say, 'Is that a proposition or a proposal?' and the answer both times before has been—"

"Both," he interrupted. "How about I tell you a little more?"

"Please."

"Stop me if I'm way out of line?"

She gestured, let's have it.

He said, "I got depressed, no good for what I did before, was transferred to a desk job, complained, it was something I hated, got transferred to the New York office, assigned to stuff which interests me."

"But of course you can't discuss it?"

"Yes."

"Meaning you can't?"

"Yes. That's true. No."

"You like Mexican? Cosme at six o'clock."

"Drinks?"

"And maybe dinner."

It was pleasant. No, really, better than that. She ordered everything she had once had with L, Tanqueray gimlets for each of them, chips and sauce, taco salad without the tacos which she could mix herself, and a shrimp ceviche and shredded beef enchilada for him. They ate everything, and had second gimlets. It was working and they knew they'd meet again, the next night and then often.

It was, however, a lengthy courtship.

She owed him so she had to keep it up, and then she wanted to keep it up. He was careful and patient with her.

The boys were uneasy when he told them, "I'm a friend of Ernie's father." The four of them, B, Betsy, Ernie and Greg, were having dinner at the Nobu on Hudson street.

Greg put his martini down. "I believe you once met my father. In a taxi on 61st Street."

"Good man, your father," B said. "Did exactly what he should have."

"But he needed to be persuaded."

B shrugged.

"Greg, please?" said Ernie. "It was years ago."

Greg smiled, said, "Good story, and he tells it well."

"You're a better man than he is," B said.

"Better lawyer maybe, one of these days," said Greg.

"That's not what I meant. Accept it."

Betsy was suddenly tearful. "Peace?"

Greg said, "Sure, Mom. Please. Drink up."

They all did.

"Something else I should tell you," B said.

Ernie said, "I hope it's something cheerful."

"It isn't."

Ernie said, "Shit. Get it over with."

"Did you know your father isn't well?" said B to Greg.

"No," said Greg.

"Nor did I," Betsy said.

"He just found out," said B. "He's planning to tell you."

"How bad?" said Greg.

B said, "I don't know. I don't have the details."

"Is that it?" said Betsy. "Can we order now?"

Ernie waved for the waiter. They ordered. The waiter left.

B was looking at Greg. Greg said, "What?"

"Something else you wanted to say?" said B.

"If I'd decided to make trouble," said Greg, "what would you have done?

Threatened me? I'd like to know. With what? And how?"

"You're family. I'd have tried to bribe you."

"How? I have money and a great job."

"A clerkship. D.C. Circuit."

"Wow."

Greg was considering it as Ernie said, "Can you really do that? How does it work?"

B said, "People do people favors."

Greg said, "Are you serious?"

B said, "You want it?"

After dinner, they summoned taxis. Two. As Betsy got into hers, Ernie said, "Oh, come on, Mom, don't be foolish. You've been together for two full years."

"Don't push it. My best to Annamarie." She closed the taxi door behind her, and off she went.

B said, "What Betsy wants she gets."

Ernie said, "What Betsy wants is foolish."

"So it goes." And he said to Greg as he boarded his cab, "Washington is international. STD's you haven't met as yet. You can't be immune to all of them."

"And sooner or later?"

"You got it." His taxi left.

Ernie said, "That guy is terrific."

Greg got the job in Washington as Second Clerk for the Chief Judge of the D.C. Circuit, starting the first day of the following month.

McAlister died the same day. Betsy took it hard, as did Irene, of course, and the two of them spent hours together. B joined them much of the time. He and McAlister had a history but of course he never explained it.

Ernie and Annamarie came down for the funeral. McAlister was cremated.

Mort had pancreatic cancer. He flew to M.D. Anderson in Houston and died there six weeks later while Greg was on his way from Washington.

Greg flew the body back to New York while B and Betsy made the funeral arrangements. Mort's three other ex-wives were hostile but they all came to the funeral. They had the service at Emanu-El and the family had a plot at Mt. Hebron. Two of the other three ex-wives came to both and so did the Chief Judge from Washington. Ernie and Annamarie came down again, and Irene sat with Betsy in the Temple. "That's what we do nowadays," said Irene. "One funeral after another."

B took Betsy to Florence and Rome for a week and to Dubrovnik and Sveti Stefan for another. "I want to see what it's like in a place where everybody hates everybody else," B said.

"Like the rest of Europe," Betsy said.

"And what we will soon have at home."

"No."

"No?" B grinned at her. "Let's talk to people in the café's," he said.

They tried hard and they did. They spent the next three days in Sveti Stefan cafes. The Serbs hated the Croats, Muslims and Albanians. There weren't many of the other three there but those who were there hated all the others.

B and Betsy fled.

They said next to nothing on the Rome-New York plane.

"At least we have each other," Betsy said.

"That's all you can have," B said.

"Family," Betsy said.

All of a sudden, she was 60.

B wanted to have a party. Ernie and Annamarie wanted to have a party. Greg and Veronica—more about that lady later—wanted to have a party. Irene wanted to have a party. Betsy did not want a party, no, no, definitely no.

They had a party with a birthday cake and sixty not just six candles. She cut it herself and ate the first piece, all of it, and everybody applauded. She lifted her champagne glass from the table and toasted, "To those who would have been invited if they could have come but are gone forever!"

"Hear hear!" everyone shouted.

Followed by a full half minute of silence.

"That's how to kill a party," she said, and there was laughter.

Ernie and Annamarie were still not married but, surprisingly, Greg was. Annamarie explained her current pro-single thinking. "I'm in advertising. The new Boston."

"What does that mean?" Betsy said.

"You'll find out."

"Isn't New York always ahead of the pack?"

"Not any more it isn't."

Betsy was digesting that, when Greg said, "Can I help you, Mom?"

Greg? What? Was this her Greg? No, it wasn't. He was totally tamed, a puppy dog, even when Veronica wasn't around. When she was, it was, "Yes, dear," "No, dear," "Please?", and "Thanks", and "Can I help?", and, even, "How can I help?"

He said to Veronica, "Yes, Princess," once, and she put down her drink,-- untouched, she wasn't drinking,-- and said back to Greg immediately, "Don't you ever say that to me, any time or anywhere, particularly in front of your mother and brother."

"What about me?" said Annamarie.

"You're included in 'brother.'"

"You must be married," said Annamarie.

"Of course," said Greg. And that's how the others found out they were. Greg continued, explaining, "She's an Assistant Attorney General of the United States."

Veronica said, "We both are, but I'm actually an Assistant Assistant."

"She takes off Fridays," Greg said.

Betsy found herself thinking, "Is this my Greg?"

That was before the announcements. There were three Veronica announcements.

Over dinner the next night, Veronica said, "Two."

"Beg pardon?" Betsy said.

"Twins," said Veronica. "I'm having twins. That's more efficient."

So that's why she wasn't drinking!

"Efficient," Betsy said.

"Yes. I'm in the fourth month, although it doesn't show. And they're girls! Both of them! Two girls. Two daughters for Greg. Delicious!" She laughed.

Granddaughers. Girls. Gregory's. That was the second announcement. Betsy's mind was reeling. She put her gimlet down. "Um. You said 'efficient'? Could you please explain?"

"In vitro. But entirely his and mine."

Annamarie laughed. "The world we live in."

That elicited Veronica's third announcement. "In case you're wondering, all ye who know him well, I know all about him."

"All?" said B, incredulous. He had been smiling but silent.

"Not all the names, but in general."

"I see," said B.

"And?" said Ernie, provocatively.

"At the slightest little suspicion, I will put him in chair, strap him down, starve him till he absolutely has to eat, cut them off and feed them to him."

Silence.

Greg said, "Sorry, Mom."

Betsy said, "Wow. Indeed. My two favorite expressions."

Veronica put her hand on Betsy's hand. "I don't want you to worry, because I won't."

"I'm not into worrying any more."

B said, "She's into grandchildren.

Betsy partially retired, working three days a week, and for others in addition to Newbury, for the new young lawyers, she preferred them. L's decorator woman was still alive and Betsy had her completely redo the apartment again, one again top to bottom. She loved it, and so did B, just the way L had previously. Her place. Her very own place, still.

"My place or yours," she and B now loved to play.

And once or twice a week, once again, "To each his own."

Next they had six years of peace and calm and visits from grandchildren. Ernie, Annamarie and Paul for a weekend every month, Greg, Veronica and the girls the next weekend, both for a week at Christmas time, and a summer month in a rented home somewhere out on the island.

Betsy worked three days a week and B worked at least part of every day at whatever he was doing. She suspected what he was doing, but. Never asked. Couldn't.

But then one night B didn't come home.

No phone call. Nothing.

She phoned his office the following morning. They were about to call her, they said. He hadn't checked in the prior evening.

She phoned his emergency line. For the first time. It didn't ring. It was silent. She phoned his office and asked them to check, please.

It had been disconnected. And no way to know where it is.

That afternoon she had visitors from both the C.I.A. and New York Police Missing Persons.

She said, "What was he doing?"

Long silence.

"Please?" she said.

The police detective finally said, "Mosques. Out in Brooklyn."

"I see," she said. "Any way to trace him?"

There was and there wasn't.

B was gone. Just like that, gone. Without a trace.

Nothing.

Ernie and Greg came and babysat for a week. Ernie stayed for a second week.

A showed up three weeks later. Arthur. He had aged. But it had been so many years.

"You've given up?" she said. "He's dead?"

"Hopefully."

"Oh."

"They're animals. Try to forget it."

She shuddered. She never could forget it.

He opened the briefcase. Gave her the papers.

She said, "Same as before?"

"I don't remember ever seeing anyone twice."

"What should I feel? Honored?" she said. She scanned the papers. They looked the same.

"One for the sole beneficiary. The other, special circumstances."

"I should feel rich but I don't," she said.

"Dear, you never spent the L money."

"I never needed any part of it."

"It's supposed to make you happy," he said. "You, not those who inherit."

"So?"

"So spend it."

Betsy thought about it. Shook her head.

"What are you going to do now?" he said. "You're reasonably wealthy."

"An elderly bereft lady."

"Think," he said.

"Can't," she said. "Maybe someday."

She tried thinking.

She gave up thinking.

She tried living without thinking.

CHAPTER FIVE

Jesus Christ. She would soon be 70.

Retirement from the firm would be mandatory. That was one of McAlister's rules and they enforced it against him.

What would her life be like with no reason to rise and shine, no place to go, not much to do, no daily contact with the business world, or its people or the big corporations, or events reported in the NEW YORK TIMES, FINANCIAL TIMES and WALL ST. JOURNAL?

She would still have the children, but they would be her life, most of it, and, if she were not careful, all of it. The boys were now visiting three times a year, and she was visiting each of them twice, but she was starting to feel like a burden. The family still rented a summer house and that was sort-of working, but the grandchildren were restless and approaching camp age and soon they would cease coming.

Even worse, no, worst of all, more and more people of the people she knew were getting sick and dying. The dead she could mourn and remember for a while, but the sick were more difficult as their illnesses were becoming more serious and the subject of endless conversation.

The latest topic was cremation. Did she want to be buried and if so, where, or fried and if so what to do with her ashes? Put them in a pot on a shelf over a fireplace, or send to the heavens in a brilliant fireworks explosion, or scatter them quietly and mournfully at some secluded spot in the ocean?

Would she die if she were always thinking about dying?

Stop. No more thinking of dying. What sort of life would it now be, living with no thought of dying?

It wouldn't be a last short installment as she had a third of her life still coming. Face it, she was healthy, thankfully, and people kept living and living, ninety, a hundred, a hundred and ten. What was that Methuselah verse in "Ain't necessarily so"? "Who calls that livin' when no gal will give in to no man who's nine hundred years?"

Maybe that's what a man is good for: company in old age and sexual gratification?

Should she go man-hunting?

If so, how?

No. No way. The hell with that. She never had and never would go man-hunting. Anyone interesting to her nowadays would likely want one of the young ones, six feet tall, blonde to her roots, twenty years old, maybe twenty-two, Russian or Eastern European.

Betsy decided to search on the internet under "life and the single mature woman."

The results were disconcerting. The first five items were cougar sites for older women wanting younger men. She had no interest in younger men and found the thought of it disgusting. Twenty-year-old boys with sixty-five-year-old women?

The next results were more promising: advice for the lonely older woman. Rule One: put yourself out there, staying at home would attract no one. That made sense, but not for her. Putting herself out there, yes, okay, but with sensible limitations. Small parties yes, events, she didn't know, bars? Bars were forty years ago. It would be like trolling for young ones.

She read on. Rule Two: only do what you want to do, and only go where you want to go, where you would find it of interest without any men. That rule was better. It spoke to her. So what would be of interest without any men, and where and when?

Magazines. She started reading them once again. There were still lots of magazines around, even if fewer people read them. Mostly young women, she decided as she page turned, it was all sex and fashion. Most of this issue was Aspen.

Mort always went to Aspen. The Little Nell in Aspen. Little Nell's, the natives called it, honoring the iconic first madam of Aspen. Well? Little Nell's for skiing? She had never skied, never wanted to ski. All that snow and cold nonsense. And now she was 70, too old to learn, even though she was in good condition.

People she knew went to Aspen. Either Florida or Aspen. Or both, for that matter, some of them. Aspen also had that summer Institute thing, June and July of every year, the very latest in idea fashion. Betsy always snickered every year when friends said they were going.

Okay. Why not? Call the Little Nell. It was early in November, so she booked a room for a month, the very next month, starting the week before Christmas. Christmas would be high season families and kids, but after New Year's they would all be gone. She told them that and they gave her a discount without any further pushing, even though Christmas was their busiest week of the year. Elated, she booked another two weeks in March and a full month in late June and July, Institute high season.

Nothing like going overboard without knowing what you are doing.

Back to the internet and a search for ski instruction+Aspen. The entries were all for Snowmass, apparently a mountain just north of Aspen. She phoned and booked an instructor for the month starting in December.

Then she phoned the children.

Greg laughed but Veronica snatched the phone and was enthusiastic and encouraging. So were Ernie and Annamarie, and Ernie called back an hour later: he had booked a five-bedroom house on Route 82 south of town, and Veronica and Greg were also coming. The grandchildren were marginally old enough for Beginners Magic Group instruction.

Whatever that was.

Betsy flew to Aspen a week before her first booking. Her ski instructor was a woman. Robin. Married to another instructor, Rex. She had lunch with Rex and Robin. She rented and a week later bought everything, skis, poles, boots, parka, pants. The lessons went well and she never fell. The prospect of falling was frightening, so Robin made her practice falling.

Then the kids arrived, all of them, all at once, and every day they all went skiing. The rented house had a huge log fireplace and a 70-inch television. They had dinner out and dinner in and on Christmas Day and New Year's Eve they had family celebrations.

Everyone left on January 4.

Betsy was surprised to find she missed them.

She was enjoying her evening gimlet on a Little Nell bar bench when the best-looking man she had seen in years seated himself in the chair across from her. "Hi," he said.

Sixties, maybe even more than that. Hair a mixture of grey and blonde. Big grin, as usual. Once again, a great, big, shit-eating grin. What did grins have to do with shit-eating?

She said, "I don't remember inviting you to sit in that chair."

"That's because you didn't."

"Then leave. Please."

He said, "You're exactly what I've been looking for."

She looked at him. Nothing. She waved to the waiter.

He said, "Don't. Please."

The waiter arrived and she said, "He sat down. I didn't invite him."

He said, "It's crowded, open seating."

"Not until five, sir," the waiter said.

"Get the house detective, please," Betsy said.

The man said, "Bitch," got up and walked out.

Hmm. Betsy watched him.

Exactly what he was looking for? That line left her wondering. What? A meal ticket, probably. And with that, she dismissed him.

She had an early dinner the following night at six o'clock in the hotel restaurant.

And guess who took the table next to her.

She asked to change tables and he said, "Please don't," but she was already standing. He said again, "Please?"

She mumbled,--stupidly, she decided afterwards,--"Promise not to talk to me, I don't want to talk, I'm thinking."

"Deal," he said.

She winced at what was not her favorite word, but sat again.

Silence. Throughout the entire meal.

When she left, he said, "Good evening."

Robin took her up the Snowmass gondola the next morning and they skied ever so slowly down Whispering Jesse and the Big Burn. Up the gondola again, then lunch at Sam's, and after lunch slowly down again. They boarded the gondola again for one last run and just as the door was closing, guess who boarded and joined them.

"Oh, come on, I'm not worth it," Betsy said.

Robin said, "You know him?"

"No, and I don't want to," Betsy said.

"You have eight minutes to make up your mind," he said.

"It's made up, I'm no one and nothing."

"No, you're not. And you haven't asked the question. You're supposed to ask the question."

"Which?"

"Why you're exactly what I've been looking for."

"A meal ticket."

"Hell, no."

Robin said, "I can ask the guys when we reach the top to throw him off the mountain."

"But you won't," he said. "And I know you can. Give me my six more minutes, Betsy."

"You know my name."

"I know lots of things. One marriage, one divorce, two sons, both married and self-supporting. Two boys and a girl grandchildren. The best paralegal in Wall Street New York, retired but missed, and might return. Comfortable but not superrich. 70 and first-time skiing."

She studied him. "How about you?"

"Guess."

"West coast education, California home, Hollywood pretty boy everything, biker, surfer, movie bits. Ten divorces from Kleenex women."

"Kleenex?"

"Take 'em, use 'em, throw 'em away."

"Actually, it's only four."

"Now please go away and leave me be."

"Without answering the question?"

"Why I'm exactly what you're looking for?"

"Yes."

"A meal ticket, I told you."

"No, ma'am. Talk."

"Talk? What kind of talk?"

"Anything but Los Angeles talk and Aspen is a Los Angeles adjunct. My name is Doyle, first name, Tim. And I'd like to give you a present. What would you like as a present?"

"Diamonds of course. A girl's best friend."

"How many carats of diamonds?"

"Ten?"

He smiled and said nothing.

The gondola reached the top and he slid out, grabbed his skis and took off, running.

Robin said, "The most ridiculous conversation I ever heard."

Betsy laughed. "Wholesale would be thirty thousand."

The package was delivered to her room at half past four that afternoon.

She unwrapped the package. Inside it was a gift-wrapped pretty box, and inside that, a plush case from Meridian. Well, he had taste, she would give him that, but Meridian was top of the line. Sensible people bought diamonds on 47th Street, wholesale, preferably, from a dealer with a good reputation.

She opened the case. The necklace took her breath away. Wow. She took two deep breaths. Ten one carat diamonds on a slender gold chain. The note read "9.83, yes I cheated, but these were close.

Dinner tonight at 7:00?" It was signed, "Tim."

No way would she take this, not from him. Not from anyone she didn't know. Certainly not from this man.

She phoned the store but they refused the return! "I'm sorry but that was the deal, ma'am," said the manager. "An estate sale, final, with a discount."

"But I can't, I don't even know the man!"

The store manager chuckled. "It's Aspen, ma'am. These things do happen."

"He's insane!"

"I'm sure. A lot of them are."

"Please," she said. "Tell me. What should I do?"

"Give it back to him."

"And if he says no?"

"Then leave it, just leave it, wherever you are."

"On a table in a restaurant?"

"If you do, let me know the restaurant."

"Thanks," she said. "Good evening."

She decided to show up at 7:20 PM, which was childish but he had it coming.

She did not apologize for being late.

He held her chair, looking at the necklace. Tim, was that his name? "Tim?" she said.

"Here we go."

"Tim, I have a big surprise for you."

"Yes, of course, I know you do."

"Oh?"

"You've decided you're going to keep it."

"You spoiled my surprise, you son of a bitch!"

"Oh, my, your language."

She started taking the necklace off, but he held up his hand, saying, "Please? At least through the dinner, please?"

The waiter arrived with gimlets for two, which he had of course ordered. She sipped hers and glared at him.

Tim grinned.

"Okay, talk," she said. "You wanted talk."

"About what? What subject? Movies, no—"

"I like movies."

"Fine, we'll get there but not off the bat, no. Politics no. Gossip no. The stock market no. Real estate no. Celebrities in Aspen no. My health no, your health no, schools no, families no, do-you-knows hell no. Does that cover the waterfront?"

"Love, sex, commitment, marriage?"

"No."

"Food?"

"May I order for both of us?"

"If I don't have to eat it."

"That's all right. I've ordered."

And he had. The waiter brought the petit plateau, oysters, clams, shrimp and crab legs for two. She said, "The most expensive first course on the menu."

It was followed by duck breast with onions and haricots verts, served with the 2011 Criots Batard Montrachet, and they finished with the watermelon three ways and the eiswein.

They ate slowly, enjoying every bite, with almost no conversation.

Betsy smiled and put her napkin on the table. "Talk?"

"Sure," he said. "What's the worst government program? What's an evil which everyone loves?"

"There are probably lots of them."

"The student loan program."

Betsy laughed. "That's ridiculous."

"Is it? College tuition keeps rising, administrative staffs are quadrupling, the salaries of professors are soaring, college presidents are paid millions. And the students are the victims."

"But kids who couldn't otherwise afford it manage to go to college, and I think that's a good thing."

"They graduate with debts, huge, obscene debts. And every year they learn less. And we've been teaching them for a hundred years that more and bigger government is the solution to pretty much everything, every real and imagined problem. Political correctness rules every campus. Academia is a hundred percent left."

"It's supposed to be, and it always was."

"They used to teach students to question."

"Some of them still do. Now and then."

"Is a college education worth it in a declining civilization? A few find jobs, very few. Managing money if they're lucky. The rest graduate knowing nothing, get jobs in media or government, or join the hundred million unemployed who don't even try to get jobs anymore and are not even counted in determining our rate of unemployment."

He stood.

She said, "And that's the lesson for the day?"

"Yes."

"I haven't said a word."

"You will? When you're ready, I know you will. Are you ready now to say what you think should be done?"

"No. So let's talk about movies?"

"What you like, and what you don't, or do you know anything about them?"

He left the restaurant.

Son of a bitch! And the necklace! She'd forgotten!

"What happened?" said Robin the following day. The very first thing the following day.

"He bought it."

"Ten carats? You're kidding!"

"Nine point eight three. On a golden chain."

"And you took it?"

"Temporarily. Meridian won't take it back."

"Oh? Meridian! How much did it cost him?"

"I never asked. But I know they're really real. I scratched the mirror in the bathroom."

"No!"

Betsy laughed. "I made that up. I didn't."

 The note said, "8:00 PM tonight?"

Should she stand him up? Go somewhere else? If she did, she would need a reservation, and he

155

would probably track her down. Better to eat alone in her room.

But what if he came knocking? She'd have to refuse to let him in.

Better in the restaurant.

She locked the necklace in the closet safe, went down early and ordered two gimlets. She was studying the menu when he arrived. She said, "How about I order and pay tonight?"

"Order yes, pay no."

"Last night cost you more than a thousand."

"So?"

"I want to pay tonight."

He shrugged and said nothing.

She ordered the snapper and the chicken. The waiter left.

Tim smiled.

She said, "Yes. The least expensive items."

"That's your privilege. You're paying. What's your favorite movie?" he said.

"No," she said. "Later. The Student Loan Program."

"Ah. You want it abolished?" he said.

"No, we can't. How do we fix it?"

"I have some ideas. Do you?"

"Yes."

"Great," he said. "Let's hear them."

"If the Education Secretary determines that in any year any common political position is seriously unrepresented on the faculty of any institution, or there has been a free speech or political correctness incident there, the number of loans to students there and the maximum amount of each such loan shall be reduced by five percent the following year."

"Spoken like a lawyer, a good one."

"A paralegal as it happens."

"Your firm should lend you to Congress to write their legislation."

"No. What I write is too succinct. Verbosity, inconsistency and vagueness are the excuses for litigation."

He laughed. "I love it."

"Well?"

"I don't know. Too political, the Secretary's determinations. Also, for openers, what's a common political position?"

"We also need a special court with exclusive and final jurisdiction over any attempt to seek review of any such determination."

"What about the federal courts of appeal? What about the Supremes?"

"No."

"Exclusive and final jurisdiction."

She nodded.

"Huh! Try and get that through Congress," said Tim.

She shrugged. "What's your program?"

"It's hopeless. I don't have one."

"So you'll let the country go down the drain with the Student Loan Program?"

"And it'll get even worse. Free college education for everyone."

"With the government of course paying."

"How do you feel about immigration?" Tim said.

"I don't," she said.

"No feeling or no opinion?"

"Neither one. We were all immigrants, or our forefathers were, but we can't afford it anymore with a hundred million unemployed, but there's no way to stop it, and it's foolish conversation."

Tim laughed and said, "So what's your favorite movie? Of all time?"

"HIGH NOON."

"Dimitri Tiomkin."

"Who?"

"The music."

"He wrote the song?"

"There's a great story which may be true. They previewed the movie without the song and it totally bombed. The critics complained about everything, Gary Cooper wanders around asking people to help, and no one but Grace Kelly does, and she's a Quaker pacifist who wouldn't, and nothing happens for an hour or more because of Foreman's really dumb screenplay and Zinnemann's slow direction. Then they dubbed the song in, and the picture was a triumph."

Betsy smiled. "And everybody won an Academy Award and the picture became the favorite of Ronald Reagan and Bill Clinton."

"Oh, for the good old days when movies were movie movies," said Tim.

"I'm not familiar with the expression."

The first course arrived. Crab cakes for two, and two glasses of the fantanel pinot grigio. He sipped, put his glass down, took a forkful of his crab cakes, held the fork and looked at her.

"What?" she said.

"I've an opening tomorrow. At six p.m. A movie."

"A movie movie?"

"I have to go."

"Is that an invitation?"

"It's at the Grauman."

"In Los Angeles?"

"I have a tiny part. A single scene."

"We could never get tickets. The planes are full."

"I'll handle that. Don't ski for a day. You need a rest."

"No, I don't need a rest."

"Well? But? Give me a but?"

"If you can get the reservations."

He booked a Lear Jet 60XR from Monarch Air. They left Aspen at 1:00

PM. They arrived in Van Nuys at 2:47 PM.

He brought chicken b-l-t sandwiches and a thermos of gimlets, and talked non-stop, takeoff to landing.

"In my less than humble opinion," he said, "the father of the movie movie was Louis B. Mayer of MGM, although he would probably have denied it. His movies tended to have three acts and an uplifting American message."

"Three acts."

"Yes. Act One introduces the main characters," he said, "at least one of whom has to be likeable, someone you'd love to bring home to meet the wife and kids, a character of sufficient interest so you're willing to spend an hour fifty-two with him at an emotional distance of six feet or less, depending on how he looks in closeup."

"And Act Two?"

"Act One has a climax. A problem the hero can't seem to solve. Something bad, something destructive. Or something or someone he wants, big time, but somehow can't possibly get it."

"Fine."

"In Act Two things get worse and worse, until everything seems totally hopeless. And Act Two is the place for subplots. If the principal story isn't rich enough, Act Two gives you subplots. Secondary characters and subplots. The Act Two climax is the emotional pits, with everything seemingly going wrong, and no way anyone can dig out of it."

"And just when everything is hopeless?"

"Act III is a determined turnaround, the struggle to the probably bitter end, but just when you have totally given up, something surprising happens, something unexpected, and the hero wins, achieving the impossible, and sending you home happy, satisfied and uplifted."

"And that's always the ending?"

"Yes. And there are five variations."

The limousine was waiting. It took them directly to the Grauman, which was now the TCL Chinese.

Tim had passes and they sat in the sixth row, but he didn't seem to know anyone. The audience was sparse for some reason.

He looked about and said, "Oh oh."

"Stinker?"

"Most movies are. But I was hoping when they had the balls to book it here that it was better than its reputation."

It started on time and it wasn't.

Tim was pretty good in his bit part, a confrontation with the heroine as a disappointed parent.

"You were good," she whispered.

He shrugged it off.

Afterwards, the limousine was waiting.

He was silent on the way to the airport, and silent when they boarded the plane.

"Go," he said to the co-pilot, and off they went.

They reached altitude, and loosened their seatbelts.

"Thank you," he said.

"For what?"

"For not talking. And for not asking if I made an investment. Which I did, of course. But I had to."

"To get the part?"

"That's normal. The script was good, initially, but there were rewrites after rewrites."

"Why rewrite, if the script was good?"

"Why do you think they make movies?"

"Good books, good stories, good script ideas, sometimes good screenplays?"

"No. Almost never."

"Explain," she said.

"A movie is a way to spend money, other people's money usually. The more people who get involved, the more money they are going to spend, some of it to make the movie, but much of it on salaries and payments to agents, managers and attorneys."

"If you say so, but why?" she said.

"Because no one knows what they are doing," he said. "It's starts with the writing. Everyone with a position has ideas he thinks are creative and he fights to get his changes made. He has a relative or a lover or a good friend whom he wants to hire for a rewrite, but rewrites don't make things better, the rewrites are simply different, as different as the rewriter can make them so the rewriter can claim he is entitled to credit and the residual and profit payments."

"So it's a mess."

"Yes. Often."

He gestured at the co-pilot. "Do you have any bourbon?"

She did her best skiing ever the following day. The sun was shining, it was actually warm, and they did eight runs, top to bottom.

Tim was cheerful at dinner the following night so she took a chance and opened it up again. "You said there were five possible endings, Five."

He smiled. "One, someone who wants something we want him to have, something he cannot possibly get, somehow gets it in a surprising way, and, even better, the villain get his comeuppance in the same way the villain has inflicted harm on others."

"Two?"

"Somebody who has been refusing to do something does it, or somebody who has in the past done something bad, does it now for a good cause. And Three, something surprising is discovered at the end that somehow makes sense of everything."

"The mind reels," she said. "Four?"

"It is going to happen all over again."

"And Five?"

"Repeating a joke for the second or third time. The audience has the joy of recognition, a chuckle at the end, and goes home with a satisfied feeling."

She shook her head. "And those are the only possibles."

"Yes, dear, that's all there are. Which one was the ending we saw last night?"

"None of them?"

"And it flopped, right?"

"Well, it wasn't one of your endings."

Tim handed her his Cross pen and the restaurant Happy Hour card. "Let me have your email. I'll let you know if I ever see a movie movie again. I can't give you my email because I don't have one any more, I'm in the process of moving."

She wrote hers on the card and handed it to him.

"Immigration?" he said. "I tried last night."

"And I passed. No point in talking."

"You have a maid?"

"A cleaning woman."

"Legal?" said Tim.

"Of course."

"And you pay the going rate, the top one."

"Yes."

"How many of your friends do?"

"Some. Many. Most, I hope."

"So who employs the illegals in New York, numbering two thirds of a million?"

"I don't know."

"Everyone."

"I thought they were living on food stamps and several kinds of unemployment."

"Seventy percent of the illegals are employed," said Tim, "compared to sixty percent of the native born and sixty of the legal foreign."

"I don't believe it. That's insane," she said.

"Those are Bloomberg's numbers and they're true today. I wanted to be sure to leave you with that as I'm leaving in the morning."

And he did. Betsy checked with the front desk before she took the Snowmass bus. Tim had checked out early in the morning.

Damn! She had forgotten to give him back his Cross pen and she still had the diamonds. She checked with hotel management but they had no valid home address, and were holding his copy of his bill till he returned. He would return, they were sure of that. He had a March reservation.

And a July reservation.

Betsy had two days of great skiing. She had a drink alone and ate alone, and slept the sleep of total exhaustion.

She phoned Arthur the next morning.

"Well, hello!" he said. "How are you?"

"I'm fine. And I must say you sound strong."

"Older but still working."

"I'm in Aspen, at the Little Nell."

"Skiing?"

"Trying. Learning. Look, I met a man who pursued me. Last name Doyle. First name, Tim. Probably Timothy but I never asked him. He took me to dinner and gave me a present. I want to return the present but he left and he said he's moving, so no address, no phone, nothing, and the hotel also has nothing except that he's driving a Lexus with California plates. Here. You might want to write it down, the license."

She read the plate digits to him.

"You want to know where to send the present."

"Yes." She paused. "Actually, I'd like to know more. Like who is he? What is he? Where is he?"

"But he's gone, he's out of your life."

"I suppose. For the present."

"You expect to hear from him again then."

"Some day, somewhere, sometime. You know the song."

"I'll have someone do some digging."

"Well, hello, there!"

It was Sandy, at the desk, checking in. Mort's friend and skiing companion. Sandy, every woman's nightmare, four wives so far and counting.

They cheek kissed.

"You're just arriving?" she said.

"Yes, how long have you been skiing?"

"A couple of weeks," Betsy said. "But I'm leaving in the morning."

"Oh, no! Please stay!" he said.

She shook her head, no. "I'm leaving in the morning."

Seriously, Sandy. No drink in the bar or dinner in the restaurant.

She was having dinner in her room when the phone rang.

"Hello?"

"It's Arthur."

"Hi. Thanks for calling."

"Sinaloa."

"That's in Mexico."

"Technically. Functionally it's independent."

"And Tim is there?"

"His car is. So he is, probably. And dear, it's not a place Americans go. He has a connection and protection."

"Oh, oh."

"And here's a strange one. His monthly American Express bill was a cool eighty-four thousand."

"That was my present, a private jet to L.A. and back, and his Little Nell statement."

"He paid American Express two days ago with a check on Chase Manhattan, and that check cleaned his Chase account down to a hundred dollar balance. If he has any more money anywhere, it's not in our banking system."

"Europe? The Caribbean?"

"If so, he hasn't filed his foreign account declaration."

"Hmm. Questions, questions, questions."

"Call me if you ever see him."

CHAPTER SIX

Betsy was once again busy. Doing much less but feeling just as busy.

She went back to Aspen for a week in March and yes, she did ski with Sandy, and she and he did have dinner, four times, with Sandy always paying, but she kept him out of her bedroom and never went near his.

And no, she never told him about Greg, although it was a great temptation. Imagine saying, out of the blue, "Hey, did you know we have a son?"

What would be his reaction? Something. But what? With Sandy you could never know.

But it wouldn't be fair to Greg, so she didn't.

What else was going on in her life? She had joined a non-NEW YORK TIMES-list book club, took it seriously and read all the books. The discussions were occasionally interesting, as was figuring out, to the extent she could, the reasons for people attending. Slightly more than half couples, a third single women, and the rest single men. Political discussions were prohibited as it was of course New York, the Democratic Party was religion and it was completely impossible nowadays to talk to its adherents; they were disciples, not merely partisans. Even the slightest deviation from the politically correct norm would elicit instant screaming and bitter ad hominem attacking. Like the unshutupable lady leftists on every channel on television.

She went back to Aspen in June for the Institute. Without Sandy, and she didn't miss him.

Charley was once again in her life. Good old Charley from her adolescence, and Betsy was sexually active once again!

Not bad for a 70-year-old woman.

There had been no sign of Tim in Aspen. She had checked with the Little Nell both times and Tim had been an unexplained no-show for both his March and June reservations.

And then in August, there he was at the Artists and Writers Game in Easthampton.

"Hi," he said. An inspiring opening.

She said, "Hello to you."

"Are you going back to Aspen?"

"The family wants to but I don't know," she said.

"The Little Nell hates me," Tim said. "I never cancelled my reservations."

And with that, he turned away, joining other people talking.

Was he going or not going? And did she care?

Would he be telephoning?

Betsy phoned Arthur on Monday morning. "Tim is in East Hampton. Or at least he was there yesterday."

Arthur now had a file on Tim. "We know what he's been doing and the source of his current funding."

"Which is what?"

"He's a coyote."

"What?"

"A coyote. An expensive one. Probably the most expensive one."

"Explanation?"

"Immigrants. Big business immigrants. Coyotes bring in the immigrants. Usually central and south Americans but in Tim's case Indians, Indians from India Indians, Hindus, never Moslems. Also Eastern Europeans, Russians, and the super-rich South Americans, Venezuelans, Colombians, Brazilians. If they get to Mexico and their cash is sufficient, he will supply them with the necessary papers and manage to find them relatives here to sponsor their immigration. Seemingly legal immigration."

"Sounds shady."

"Maybe. Sometimes. But they have money and provide employment. They fund and front restaurants. In which our Timmy takes ten or twenty percent. Without a cash investment."

"And all of this is recent?"

"He started in 2007."

"But somehow you never heard of him."

"He kept under the radar. San Diego, Los Angeles, Portland, Denver, Dallas, Houston, Austin."

"And now New York?"

"No, New Jersey, not New York. Passaic, Lyndhurst, North Bergen."

"Never been there, never heard of them."

"Let me know next time you see him."

There was something strange about the conversation but Betsy decided not to dwell on it. Tim hadn't called her so the hell with him.

She booked Aspen again at Christmas time, and so did the family. Sandy, too, and that might be a problem, as Ernie knew about Sandy and Greg, as she had long ago told him. Ernie might not like seeing Sandy, or wondering about his mother and Sandy again, so she made no plans to see Sandy until after the kids were leaving.

It was all even more successful than it had been the previous season, but this year it was cold, too cold, so she went back to New York on January 7, after rebooking for a full two weeks in March of Sandy and spring skiing.

Betsy's telephone was ringing. The clock said 9:15. Which was late for her, but oh, she was home, in her New York apartment, and it was 7:15 in Aspen. Charley was in bed beside her. He had picked her up at La Guardia and. She smiled, remembering the "and". The before and after as well as the during.

She picked up the telephone. "Good morning?"

"It's the desk, ma'am. There's a gentleman here wants to speak to you. May I put him on?"

"Yes, of course."

The second voice said, "Good morning."

"Arthur?"

"May I come up? It's urgent."

"Sure, just give me a moment." Betsy got out of bed and scrambled for her bathrobe. It was draped over a chair.

Charley was standing. "You want me dressed and out of here or hiding in the bathroom?"

"Fool, just put your pants on."

The doorbell buzzed. Betsy trotted off to answer it.

Charley called after her, "That wasn't much of a moment."

Arthur entered and he and Betsy cheek-kissed, as always, never a hug, just a cheek-kiss. He went past her to the dining room table, took a map out of his briefcase and spread it out.

Charley appeared.

Betsy said, "This is Charley."

Arthur said, "Yes, I know."

Betsy started to introduce them. "Charley, this is Arthur." To Arthur, she said, "Do you want him here?"

"Yes, he can be helpful." To Charley he said, "Mind doing something for your country?"

Charley was silent.

Arthur was leaning over the map. "Look."

It was Manhattan and north New Jersey.

Arthur said, "Member what I told you? About his restaurants? Passaic, Lyndhurst, North Bergen? And you never heard of any of them?"

"I have," said Charley. "I follow the Giants. Football. The MetLife Stadium."

"So?" said Betsy.

"You don't get it," Arthur said.

"The football game Sunday?" Charley said. "The Stadium holds 90,000."

"Crowded together and cheering," Arthur said.

Charley said, "Who is "his" and what about restaurants?"

"A friend of Betsy's, sort of, whom she once met in Aspen, brings people in from overseas and sets them up in restaurants."

"Tim Doyle," said Betsy. "But I haven't seen him since August in East Hampton. He hasn't phoned me, not even once, and he wasn't at the Nell in Aspen."

"He's having dinner at the Sherry-Netherlands at eight o'clock tonight and Charley has a reservation. Table for two."

"The Cipriani," Charley said.

"That one."

"What do you want us to do and say?"

"I don't know," said Arthur. "Something. Anything. Try to get him talking. What?"

Betsy said, "He once gave me an argument about illegal immigration."

"Good. Be against it. Fight with him. Fight with the people with him. All of them will be foreign. Maybe they'll drop something, say something."

"The room is bugged?" said Charley.

"The tables, his, yours."

Betsy said, "There's something missing."

Arthur took more papers from his briefcase. Put them on the table. Betsy and Charley looked at them. "What is it?" Betsy said. "A cannon?"

"It's the M119. Our lightweight howitzer, 105 millimeter, crew of five, eight rounds a minute, a twelve mile range."

"Where do we keep them?" Charley said.

"The Tenth Mountain Division up in Vermont has them, but one is out for repair and missing. The Saudis have a dozen and several of those may be missing. Somebody ran a test in Mexico last month of some sort of mortars or howitzers and those are now missing."

190

"And they may be in the restaurants? What the hell, go get them!" Charley said.

"We don't have enough for a search," Arthur said. "One of the joys of the Fourth Amendment."

"Fuck that noise," said Charley. "With 90,000 lives at stake? I have friends, we'll go tonight, give me the three locations."

Arthur said, "We need you more in the Sherry Netherlands."

Cipriani. There were flowers on their table and Betsy was partially obscured behind them. She and Charley were studying their menus when Charley said, "Showtime."

"How many with him?"

"Two men and a hijabbed woman."

191

The headwaiter seated Tim and his party at the very next table. Tim thanked the headwaiter, sat, and reacted to the sight of Betsy as she said, "Tim?"

He rose and kissed her cheek. Betsy introduced Charley. "Tim, this is Charley. Charley, Tim."

Charley half rose and Tim smiled as they shook hands. "Not quite a friend, more an acquaintance," said Tim. "The Little Nell in Aspen."

"We argued a lot," Betsy said.

"Politics?" said Charley.

"Movies," said Tim.

"Student loans," said Betsy. "And immigration. Are your friends there immigrating?"

"Hardly," said Tim. "Just visiting."

"No introductions?" Betsy said.

Tim made a face.

"I'm all for immigration," Charley said. "I have restaurant investments. Waiters, dishwashers, clean up help, I'd be lost without them."

"Me, too," Tim said.

"In what way?" Betsy said.

"I have restaurants."

"Me, too," Betsy said. "I have a piece of Charley's. I sold the necklace and made the investment."

"Oh." Tim started to turn away.

"Where are yours?" Charley said. "Let us know. We'll give 'em a try."

"They're not exactly convenient," said Tim. "New Jersey. North Bergen."

"That's great!" said Charley. "We'll be there Sunday, you know, for the game. Who shall we call for a reservation?"

Tim hesitated, then produced a card. "I don't know, you might not like the food. Mexican, Indian, Caribbean. Here. Call me, I'll give you the locations."

"I will."

"Good to see you, Tim," Betsy said.

Tim rejoined his companions.

Arthur was in Betsy's apartment and about to leave.

"You heard it?" said Charley.

"All of it. You did your best," Arthur said. "Particularly your telling him you were going."

Betsy said, "That caused some hesitation."

"A moment at most," Arthur said.

Charley said, "So now what happens?"

"I'm on my way," Arthur said. "I have people waiting."

"For what?"

"Each gun is five by six by sixteen feet." Arthur said. "Storage requires a good sized room, a garage, an attic or a basement. Three crews for the three locations, 4:00 AM."

"You're going in tonight?" Charley said.

"I didn't hear that question."

Arthur left.

At 6:00 AM Betsy's phone rang.

Charley pounced, picked it up, handed it to her.

She said, "Hello?"

"It's me. We drew a blank."

"Nothing," Betsy said to Charley.

He reached for the phone. "Idea," he said.

"Please," Arthur said.

"I looked it up on the internet. Each of those howitzers, or mortars, or whatever they are, needs a crew of five to seven. That's fifteen to thirty foreign men, a lot for a New Jersey neighborhood, and they must be clustered in groups somewhere. Hotels, motels, bed and breakfast homes, empty houses available for lease short terms. Mark off a radius of five miles, pi times the radius squared is seventy-five square miles. It shouldn't take that long to comb seventy-five square miles, and somebody might have seen them."

"Good idea," said Arthur. "What do you do? Hospital administration?"

"Keep us posted?" Charley said.

"I will."

Friday passed. All day, nothing. Charley called in sick and stayed in the apartment.

Saturday, all day, nothing.

Betsy phoned Arthur at 4:00 pm.

"Yes?"

"Charley has another idea."

"Put him on."

Charley took the phone. "They're not there, and the men aren't there. They're in box trucks, twenty-footers. They could be a hundred miles away, four hundred, eight hundred miles away. The restaurants are parking lots. Places to stop. There are other places to stop of course but the restaurant lots would be perfect."

"We're looking for other places to stop."

Charley said, "You need attack helicopters, gunships, hovering over the roads within five or ten miles, starting at noon tomorrow."

"Six."

"Six what?"

"Six gunships," Arthur said. "They gave us six gunships."

"That's all? For seventy-five square miles?"

"We'll have twenty-two police cars. Starting at five o'clock in the morning, and swarming the area everywhere, all roads and likely places to park."

"Can you block all the roads, say, ten miles out? Or at least set up roadblocks?"

"The game, man. We can't block traffic to the game."

"Shit."

Betsy took the phone. "We'd like to stay involved. Can we stay involved?"

Charley was excited. "In a gun ship?"

Arthur laughed. "No way. How about your place? That may work. I can be there Sunday at 6:00 a.m. Will that work for you?"

Betsy said, "Let's do it."

On Sunday morning at 5:30 a.m., Charley went out for donuts, plain and cinnamon, a dozen of each, while Betsy made the coffee.

Charley came back with Arthur at ten to 6:00. Betsy had spread the map on the dining room table. Arthur had brought phones and a speaker. They were on their second cups of coffee at half past six, saying little, and starting to feel a little foolish, when the phone rang; they had scored their first hit! The Jersey City police had stopped a Morgan 20-footer crossing the Passaic River going north on 95!

Arthur was shouting into the phone, "Search it! Search it!"

They did, and bingo! The stopped box truck contained the missing Vermont M119 and a crew of six who insisted that they were the mechanics from Anniston, Alabama who had repaired the howitzer and were now returning it to the Tenth Mountain Division in Vermont.

They had no explanation for their truckload of thirty high explosive HERA M913's.

"Then it's for real!" said Betsy. She was aghast.

Arthur was on his second phone, demanding an additional ten gunships.

Charley was studying the map. "The next one will be coming south," he said, "on 17, Interstate 80, 21 or 19."

Arthur repeated that into the telephone and joined Charley over the map. "What about another going north," Arthur said, "on the Garden State Parkway or 21? Or west to east on 3?"

"I don't know," Charley said. "It seems to me that east is blocked, because that's where Manhattan is, and most of the game traffic will be coming from there, so south, north and then west. South, west, north is too logical."

"Logical."

"Yes."

Arthur shook his head.

"Okay, it's a guess."

The phone rang again at 8:15 AM. Bingo 2, another Morgan! The

Hackensack Police had spotted it coming down Interstate 80 and turning south on 17. Eight Canadians, including the driver, one M119, and thirty more high explosive HERA M913's. The Canadians refused to talk and were carted away.

Charley kept talking.

"Two more thoughts," he said. "The Teterboro Airport is an obvious place to park and let the stadium have it, so let's keep it under observation all the time. Tell the gun ships to refuel there."

"That's one thought. What's the other?" Arthur said.

"One was coming south to north, the second one was coming north to south, so let's look for the other two coming west to east, a pair of trucks together, and not Morgans. Chevies, Fords, Penskes, Nissans. West to East on 280 or 3."

Arthur repeated that into the telephone.

But: 9:00 AM. Nothing.

10:00 AM. Nothing.

"What if they hit the crowd early?" Betsy asked.

"They won't, no way," said Charley.

"Charley the mind reader," Betsy said.

"Don't," said Arthur.

"Sorry," she said.

A call came in at 11:30 AM. There were two International Durastar 4300 24-footers heading east on 3 just east of the Garden State Parkway. An hour out. More than an hour. Plus setup time. Stop or wait?

"Stop! Immediately!" said Arthur.

The New Jersey State Police did.

Three of the gunships hovered overhead.

Crews of six in one, seven in the other, each with an M119, and thirty high explosive HERA M913's. No explanation, no talking, and carted away.

Huge deep breaths and sighs of relief. "Champagne?" said Betsy.

"I'm game," Arthur said.

Charley said nothing.

Betsy had a 60-inch TV and she and Arthur sipped champagne and watched the game on television.

Charley was not drinking. His glass was full, beside him on the dining room table. He was poring over the map.

Arthur joined him and said, "What?"

Charley said nothing.

"Something we missed?" said Arthur.

"Worse."

"What could possibly be worse?"

"Another one. At half time."

"Think," said Charley. "What is missing?"

"Nothing," said Arthur. "We got all four."

Charley traced the four routes on the map. "South to north, we got them. North to south, we got them. West to east, two, we got them."

"Four out of four."

"So?"

"There's another."

"How so?"

"It's like chess. Do you play?"

"No."

Charley was hesitant. "The restaurants were cover, for him and his people to be there, to be seen in the neighborhood. They were not a place for M119 storage. That was stored somewhere else, long ago, before he opened the restaurants. And his crew are not in a boarding house, a motel, or an empty rental. And there are only five or six of them, each living in his own place in Newark or Manhattan. And the trucks were a diversion."

"Diversions plural," Arthur said. "Expensive diversions."

"The restaurant staffs all headed to work today, at the usual time for each of them, eleven o'clock this morning. Only some of them never got there, the M119 crew didn't."

 "So where are they? How do we find them?

"It's needle in a haystack time. Look. Where would you put them?

"Dunno," said Arthur.

"East of there is my guess," Charley said.

Arthur was on the telephone. "All sixteen of the gunships! In the air and keep them there! Focus? Everywhere. Open spaces. Parking lots. North, West, South, Eastern."

Betsy joined them. "Half time."

Arthur was on the phone again. "Now! They're rolling it out in the open!"

One minute. Nothing.

Two minutes. Nothing.

Three—and the voice on the speaker said, "The Izod Center parking lot, behind the Racing Commission."

The sound on the speaker was deafening. "Two, three, five gunships, hovering, landing! State Police on Washington Avenue! Arena Road! Got 'em!"

The Giants won.

The crowd left the Meadowlands.

Tim's restaurants filled to capacity, as if nothing at all had happened.

Arthur was leaving.

"Where is Tim?" Betsy asked him.

"Havana last night, Spain this morning."

Charley laughed.

Arthur said, "How old are you?"

"Seventy-two."

"Retired? Collecting a pension?"

"Why?"

"You have a talent."

"For guessing?"

"For whatever it is. I know it when I see it and I get it when I can." Arthur

208

handed Charley a business card. "I work six days a week, mornings."

Arthur and Betsy hugged and Arthur left.

Betsy said, "I was thinking of doing some traveling."

"Alone?" said Charley.

"With you."

"The job might be fun."

"It would be fun. Working for Arthur is great fun. L said it often. B, too."

"New York is a problem," Charley said.

"A dangerous place."

"Every place is dangerous nowadays. Big cities, certainly. Every one."

"Noo Yawk, Noo Yawk," Betsy said. "My town, our town."

Charley said, "It isn't our old Noo Yawk any more. It's different. Our world is different. Anyhow, I hate the accent."

"So?"

"So I'm your man, Betsy, dear. It took a while, but here we are. I'm yours and you're mine."

Betsy smiled.

"What?"

"Am I a silver dollar?" she said.

"Like the song?"

"'Just like a silver dollar goes from hand to hand, a woman goes from man to man?'"

"Oh, no! You're not silver, love of my life. You're not silver. You're gold. Pure golden."

Made in the USA
Middletown, DE
16 October 2023